"I believe you promised me this dance."

A deep, sexy male voice slid down her spine like a smooth cognac.

Valentina glanced up and saw a tall, broad-shouldered man wearing a black Stetson and a tux, his blue eyes searing into hers.

"Yes, I did."

When he pulled her against him, his hard-muscled frame made something inside shudder and relax at the same time. From the moment she'd been born, Princess Valentina had been bred for duty. Her position was more important than her desires. She was always to behave responsibly.

"I don't want this night to end," he said, pulling her closer.

Clearly he knew what he wanted and, for this moment, she knew that he was what she wanted.

"Me, neither," she said, and lowered his mouth to hers.

Responsibility would have to wait.

Dear Reader,

Do you know anyone who does so much for others that they forget to take care of themselves? They're so busy doing their job that they forget what they need. They forget what they really want. Because, surely whatever they want can't be as important. Hmm. Maybe you are that person sometimes?

I loved heroine Valentina Devereaux from the moment she sprang into my mind and heart. The poor girl works like a dog, deals with a pain-in-the-butt-brother-prince and younger siblings who whine and shirk their duties at every turn. Okay, so the truth is this could be any family.

Princess Tina takes a break from being a princess for just one night and gives in to what she wants, and oh, boy, does that night turn the world upside down. Her instincts lead her to the one man who could make everything in her world right. Maybe… You'll find out soon enough….

Enjoy,

Leanne Banks

ROYAL HOLIDAY BABY

LEANNE BANKS

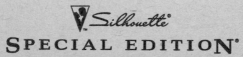

Published by Silhouette Books

America's Publisher of Contemporary Romance

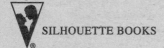 SILHOUETTE BOOKS

Recycling programs
for this product may
not exist in your area.

ISBN-13: 978-0-373-65557-1

ROYAL HOLIDAY BABY

Visit Silhouette Books at www.eHarlequin.com

Printed in U.S.A.

Books by Leanne Banks

Silhouette Desire

*The Royal Dumonts
†The Billionaires Club
**The Medici Men

LEANNE BANKS

is a *New York Times* and *USA TODAY* bestselling author who is surprised every time she realizes how many books she has written. Leanne loves chocolate, the beach and new adventures. To name a few, Leanne has ridden on an elephant, stood on an ostrich egg (no, it didn't break), gone parasailing and indoor skydiving. Leanne loves writing romance because she believes in the power and magic of love. She lives in Virginia with her family and four-and-a-half-pound Pomeranian named Bijou. Visit her Web site at www.leannebanks.com.

Thank you, Gail.

Chapter One

Tina adjusted her mask and breathed a sigh of relief. The masquerade party was in full swing with the house band slipping into a hip-hop number. For the next two hours, she could be anyone she wanted to be. In her case, that would be anyone other than the older sister of Her Highness Fredericka Anna Catherine of the small kingdom of Chantaine.

Thank God her college friend, Keely, had invited her to Dallas to celebrate her daughter's christening and catch up. Tina couldn't bear any more of the pitying glances she received when people talked about her beautiful younger sister's marriage to a wealthy Parisian film director. It was all so glamorous, so exciting, and while she was happy for her sister, she was sick of everyone asking when she was getting married. After all, she was older than Ericka and the event had stirred up her brother's suggestion that Tina should marry someone who could aid in Chantaine's political interests.

But she wasn't going to think about that tonight. Tonight

the only person who knew her true identity was dancing with her husband at the other end of the room. Keely caught her glance and waved.

Tina waved in return, glad to see her friend enjoying a night out with her hubby.

"Wanna dance?" a man said.

She glanced up, surprised at the invitation. "Oh, no, thank you very much. I'm enjoying watching right now."

"Maybe a drink would help you loosen up," he suggested.

A little pushy, she thought and gave him a once-over. He stood about an inch shorter than her in heels. She didn't like his slicked-back hair or his voice. It was whiny sounding.

Tina had always had a weakness for a sexy voice, though she'd kept that to herself. She shook her head. "No, thank you. Excuse me, I see a friend," she fibbed and moved away.

She accepted a crab cake appetizer from one waiter. Another offered her a glass of champagne. Seconds later, Keely appeared by her side. "How's it going? Are you sure you don't want me to introduce you around?"

"Absolutely not," Tina said. "I'm ecstatically anonymous."

"If you're sure," she said in the warm friendly twang that had welcomed Tina since they first became roommates in college. "I guess it's nice not to have to put on your princess face."

Tina felt a twinge of guilt. She knew her position carried both benefits and responsibilities and she'd tried to never shirk from her duties, but lately it had felt overwhelming. "Just a little break," she said. "I'll be headed back to Chantaine day after tomorrow. I can't tell you how much I've appreciated having this time with you."

"We've loved having you," Keely said. "Are you sure you can't stay a little longer?"

Tina shook her head. "No. Remember, the wedding takes place in two months."

Keely shot her a look of sympathy. "Duty calls. You're always giving up what you want for others, Tina. One of these days you're going to rebel and shock everyone."

Tina laughed. "Not likely. Someone's got to toe the line in Chantaine and it looks like it's going to be me." Uncomfortable with the discussion, she pointed to the dance floor. "As you would say, time's a wasting. Enjoy your time with your husband."

Keely gave a mocking dip of her head. "Yes, your highness, but there's no reason you can't kick up your heels yourself. If a gorgeous guy asks you to dance, promise me you'll do it," she whispered.

"I don't know," Tina said, thinking of the man who'd approached her earlier.

"Promise," Keely said.

"Oh, okay," Tina relented, because she knew there wasn't much of a possibility for such a thing happening. "But he has to be gorgeous."

"Agreed," Keely said and left to drag her husband out on the dance floor.

Tina took a step back and observed the crowd. She enjoyed the novelty of being the observer rather than the observed. To her left, she heard a group of men discussing the fate of the Dallas Cowboys. To her right, she noticed a man seductively feeding his date an appetizer. Feeling a strange stab of envy at the romance oozing from them, she immediately looked away.

When had a man wanted her just because she was a woman, just because she was herself, instead of wanting her because she was Princess Valentina Catherine Marie of Chantaine? Try never, she thought and immediately felt frustrated with herself. She led an amazing life. Why had she been so dissatisfied lately?

"Let me take you on the dance floor," the man who'd approached her earlier said. "I can show you a good time."

Be careful what you wish for, she told herself, but this was not the guy of her dreams. She sighed. "No, again," she said firmly. "But thank you."

His hand on her arm took her off guard. "No need to be so shy. We could have some fun."

"No, thank you," she said, pulling back her arm and frowning when he didn't release her. She didn't want to make a scene, but this man was making things difficult. In other circumstances, her security detail would handle this, but tonight she'd successfully ditched them. She hadn't done that since college.

"I'm really not interested—"

"Excuse me," she heard another man say. A deeper, sexier male voice slid down her spine like the smoothest cognac in the history of the world.

She glanced up and saw a tall, broad-shouldered man with black hair wearing a black Stetson, a black mask and a tux. "I believe you promised this dance to me," he said, his blue eyes searing into hers through the slits of the mask.

Tina's heart tripped over itself. She met his gaze and felt an instant inexplicable trust and attraction. She gave it a second thought, then dismissed it. "Yes, I did," she said and accepted the hand he offered.

"Well, I guess," the whiny-voiced man began.

The lone ranger, however, led her onto the dance floor and guided her into a slow dance to a romantic song. "It looked like he was causing you trouble."

"I suppose so," she said, hyper-aware of his strong chest and clean, musky scent.

"Should I not have interrupted?" he asked.

"No," she said then corrected herself. "I mean yes." She swallowed a groan.

His hard mouth lifted into a slight grin. "Which is it? Yes or no?"

"Both," she said, stiffening her spine. "He was causing me trouble, but I should have handled it."

He spun her around then drew her back against him. "Now you don't have to."

She couldn't help smiling. "So I don't."

Tina danced through another song with the mysterious stranger, then the band took a break and he lifted her hand to his lips. "Maybe later," he said and moved away. The crowd closed behind him like the Red Sea.

Tina looked around for him but couldn't see him.

Keely appeared in front of her. "I'm sorry, sweetie, but the babysitter called and Caitlyn won't stop crying. Brent and I are going home."

"I'll go with you," Tina said.

"Absolutely not," Keely said with a firm shake of her head. "This is your last chance to have fun for a while. We've already asked a friend to look after you."

Tina cringed. "That's not necessary."

"It's either that or your security," Keely said. "There's no need for you to leave now."

Tina thought of the handsome man who'd danced with her earlier. Why not? "Okay. But I'll probably get to your house in less than an hour."

"Don't rush. Remember, you've got Ericka's wedding coming toward you like a freight train."

The very thought exhausted her. "Okay, you've convinced me."

"Hey," Keely said. "The crab cakes are great."

Tina laughed and gave Keely a hug. "Go home and comfort your baby."

"Yeah, yeah," Keely said then pulled back. "Call me if you need me."

As Tina watched her friend walk away, she felt a combination of exhilaration and terror. She was officially all alone at a party. Except for Keely's mysterious friend.

Zachary Logan watched the brown-haired beauty accept a glass of champagne from the tray the waiter offered her. She also accepted a crab cake.

He smiled to himself. He liked a woman with an appetite. His good friends Keely and Brent McCorkle had asked him to look after Tina Devereaux. The only thing he knew about the woman was that she was Keely's guest from out of town. He owed Brent a favor so he would do what his good friend asked despite the fact that he had been counting the seconds until he could escape this party.

Zach had been cajoled into attending this party by both friends and relatives. It had been two years since his Jenny and their baby had died, and he'd gone into seclusion at his ranch outside of Fort Worth. The pain of his loss still stabbed at him, the memories gutting him like a fish.

For the first time, the gaiety of the social gathering lifted his spirits, and Tina flat-out made him smile. Full-figured, with good manners and an accent he couldn't quite place, she looked at him with a feminine curiosity that grabbed at him and drew him.

She took a sip of bubbly, then licked her lips and he felt an odd twist in his stomach. With the mask covering much of her face, it was easy to focus on her full, puffy mouth, the color of a deep rose. Soft and sensual looking. He rubbed his thumb over his own mouth, feeling a slight buzz.

He shook his head at himself. Where had that thought come from? Noticing how she tapped her toe to the music, he took the hint and walked toward her.

"Another dance?" he suggested, extending his hand.

Her green eyes lit up. "That would be nice," she said and looked around for a place to put her glass. He took it from her and nodded toward a waiter who came to collect it, then led her onto the dance floor.

She shimmied to a dance club tune, laughing throughout the song as if she were getting away with something. Her attitude was contagious and he caught himself smiling more than he had in months. The song blurred into another and another until a slow tune began and he pulled her into his arms.

"I just realized I don't even know your name," she said. "I'm Tina."

"Zach," he said. "Zach Logan."

"I would have never expected it, but this is the most fun I've had in—" She paused, a surprised look coming over her face. "Forever," she confessed.

He chuckled. "Maybe you're like me. Maybe you need to get out more."

"Oh, I get out," she said. "Just not like this. I hate to see it end, but I need to leave before the big reveal."

"What do you mean?" he asked.

"I need to leave before everyone takes their masks off at the end of the evening."

"Why? Do you want your identity to remain secret?"

She shot him a cautious glance and shrugged. "Something like that." The music stopped and she started to pull away. "I should go. Thank you, Zach Logan."

He couldn't let her leave on her own. He'd promised Keely and Brent he would make sure she got home safely. "Let me take you," he said. "Can't have a beautiful woman like you leaving by herself. And I know a place close by that serves the best ice cream floats if you're interested."

She looked tempted. "I shouldn't," she said, her voice oozing reluctance.

"Why?" he challenged, not eager for the evening to end either. He would go back to his apartment, full of memories that reminded him of how much he'd lost. "It's just ice cream with a local boy."

"Boy," she echoed in breathless disbelief, giving him a once-over.

"Okay," he amended. "It's just ice cream."

"Well, you did rescue me from that creep," she said, caught in indecision. She squished her eyes together for a half beat then opened them. "I really shouldn't get into a car with a man I've just met."

"I can get you a cab," he said.

"Thank you," she said, disappointment leaking through her tone. He escorted her to the door of the private club and waited with her while the valet waved a car forward.

He opened the door and just before she stepped inside, she glanced over her shoulder. "I could still meet you for that ice cream float if I knew the address."

"Calahan's Diner on 54th and Poplar," he said to the driver and her. "See you soon."

Forty-five minutes later after Tina removed her mask, she sat across from the rugged man with the magnetic eyes. "I can't remember the last time I had one of these," he said as he drained the last drop.

Her gaze slid down his hard jaw, taking in the slide of his Adam's apple, then lower to his broad shoulders. Watching him drink the float was the most seductive experience she'd had in a long time.

Tina wondered if that was just plain pathetic as she took another sip of her own float. She liked the way his bedroom eyes crinkled at the corners. The fact that he was knocking back an ice cream float made him seem a little less dangerous than if he'd been swilling whiskey. She supposed that if she were ever going to do something wild and impetuous with a man, he might be a good choice. Not that she ever would.

"You never mentioned where you live," he said.

"Out of the country, right now," she said. "But I attended college at Rice."

"Is that where you met Keely?" he asked.

Tina blinked, digesting his comment and what it meant. She felt a rush of self-consciousness. "You were the one Keely asked to look after me."

He nodded and his lips tilted into a half smile. "My pleasure."

She resisted the urge to fan her heated face. "This is a little embarrassing. I didn't know you were assigned to look after me. I shouldn't keep you any longer—"

His smile fell. "No," he said. "When I said it was my pleasure, I meant it. I haven't been out in awhile. Being with you has—" He broke off and shrugged those broad muscular shoulders. "It's been great. I haven't felt this good in a long, long time."

His eyes darkened with emotion, and she felt a visceral tightening in her stomach.

"I don't want it to end," he said.

His words echoed her own feelings. She sucked in a quick breath, determined to clear her head. She had responsibilities. Her duty was most important. Always. "I don't either, but it must end." She closed her eyes for a quick moment, trying to stiffen her resolve. Opening her eyes again, she shot him a smile that she knew was weary. "Grown-ups have to be grown-ups."

He nodded, giving a slight chuckle as he slid his gaze over her from head to waist, heating her from head to toe. "Damn shame, isn't it?"

"Yes," she said, wishing she were a little less responsible, wishing she could be impetuous and follow her heart...or hormones....

"I'll get the check, then get you a cab," he said.

Moments later, she sat in the back of a cab driving her toward Keely's house. Damn chivalry, she thought and gave a dark laugh at herself. It would have been so much easier if he'd taken advantage of her. Oozing his sexy Texan charm, it would have been sooo easy. Instead, he'd given her a choice, which meant she'd had to take the chaste high road when she'd wanted to be a bad girl. Just once. She'd always been the good daughter. At the moment, that halo she wore felt way too tight.

The taxi stopped at a red light. When it turned green, the vehicle sputtered and stalled. Great, she thought. She was accustomed to riding in perfectly maintained limousines. Riding in a taxi was an adventure. Under a torrential downpour, she looked outside her window and hoped the cab would start.

The driver cranked the engine again. And again. And again. To no avail.

Darn it, she didn't even have an umbrella with her. Her staff usually provided that. Tina sighed. Perhaps she should call her security. Heavens, she hated the idea. There would be a fuss from the head of security and her brother and maybe even her father.

She waited several more moments, her cell phone ready in her hand. An SUV pulled alongside the cab. A moment later, a knock sounded at her window, startling her. Frightened, she stared into the rain, reluctant to open her door.

"Tina," a male voice said. "Open up."

Recognizing the voice of Zachary Logan, she opened the door. "Zach," she said.

His Stetson dripping with raindrops, he swung an umbrella toward her. "Need a ride?"

"To where?"

His gaze gave a dark flicker. "Wherever you want. I can take you to Keely's or I can take you to my place in town."

Tina stared into his eyes and felt as if she were balanced on a precipice. She could be sensible or cautious or for once, give into her passions. She saw a ravenous need in Zach's gaze that called to something inside her. She'd been taught to ignore her needs. But somehow, the tug she felt toward Zach was stronger than anything she'd ever felt before.

Tina rose from the cab with all the grace she'd been taught since she could walk and accepted his hand. "Your place," she whispered.

Chapter Two

Tina stepped across the threshold of Zach's apartment, her heart hammering in her chest. When Zach flicked on the light behind her, she stared into the spare, generically furnished living space and felt her stomach dip with reticence. What was she doing?

"Let me get you something to drink," he said, walking past her and removing his hat. "Sorry I don't have much to offer. I spend most of my time working when I stay here instead of at my ranch."

She followed after him and watched as he stared into a near-empty refrigerator. "Juice, water." He craned his neck. "Beer and chardonnay."

"Water's fine," she said, licking her lips.

"Sure you don't want wine?" he asked, looking over his shoulder.

"Maybe just one glass," she said. "Besides ranching, what kind of business do you have?"

Zach grabbed a beer, then opened the bottle of wine and poured the golden liquid into a glass. "My brother and I own some companies together—information-sharing systems and upgrading equipment for mid-size companies. We also offer consultation for trading futures and trade them ourselves."

"Sounds busy," she said and accepted the glass of wine.

"What do you do?"

"I work in public and international relations," she said, not wanting him to ask any further questions. She took a quick sip and stared into his gaze, feeling her stomach dance with nerves.

He skimmed his gaze over her, then took a long drink of beer. "Listen, if you'd like me to take you to Keely's—"

"No," she said, quickly, breathlessly. "Unless you want me to go."

"No," he said just as quickly, but his voice was rougher with a sensual edge to it that affected her on a visceral level.

She took another sip of wine and willed herself to be more brazen. She took two steps forward then stopped. "I'm not accustomed to making the first move," she whispered.

He raised his eyebrows and nodded, taking another long drink of beer. "Maybe I can help with that," he said and closed the space between them.

Inhaling deeply, she caught the scent of him, soap, cologne and just a hint of musk. He smelled male, good, seductive. He slid his hand over hers and tugged her toward the kitchen counter where he propped his can of beer.

His hand felt strong and warm around hers. Taking her wine glass from her hand, he took a quick sip, then also set the glass on the counter. He dipped his fingers into the wine and rubbed them over her lips.

She blinked at the raw seductive move, but had no desire to object.

"I think I need another taste of that wine," he said and

lowered his mouth to hers. His mouth was firm and sensual. He slid his tongue over her lips and she felt his hunger vibrate inside her. When he pulled her against him, his hard-muscled frame made something inside shudder and relax at the same time.

She wasn't dealing with a college boy here.

She remembered her first time as heavy kisses, awkward fumbling, a rushed penetration followed by a stab of pain. Afterward, she'd wondered *Why bother?*

Tina knew she was experiencing the opposite side of the spectrum. Zachary was a man, and he clearly knew what he was doing. He knew what he wanted and at this moment, she knew that he was what she wanted. From the time she'd been born, Tina had been bred for duty and responsibility. Her position was more important than her desires or personal needs. She was always to behave responsibly. If things went wrong, then she was supposed to fix them. She would always need to remain on guard.

For the first time in a long time, if not forever, she let down her guard. She had the bone-deep sense that Zach was the most responsible man she'd ever met. For now, his responsibility meant taking care of his needs and her own, and she felt a delicious anticipation that he could achieve both tasks. She sighed with a combination of relief and excitement and clung to his strong frame.

Giving herself into his sensual care, she drew his tongue into her mouth, savoring his taste. He quickly inhaled in surprise or approval, or both, and rocked her pelvis against his hardness.

A thrill raced through her and she pressed her breasts against his chest. He gave a low growl. "Are you sure you—"

"Yes," she whispered desperately against his lips and slid her hands upward, knocking his hat from his head.

Within seconds, he had pushed off her coat and unzipped her dress. Tina felt a draft of cool air when her dress pooled at her feet, but his warm hands replaced the fabric, quickly distracting her. She tugged at his jacket and tie then fumbled as she unbuttoned his shirt.

It seemed like both forever and no time at all before she felt his naked warm skin against hers. The sensation of her breasts against his chest made her nipples tight with need. Heat and desperation grew inside her. When had she wanted like this? When had she allowed herself to want like this?

Her brain shorted out as he dipped his head, taking one of her nipples into his mouth. Tina gasped in pleasure.

He swore under his breath. "You're so sexy. Don't know how long I can wait."

"Don't," she urged, sliding her fingers through his hair. "Don't wait."

Taking her by surprise, he pulled her into his arms and carried her out of the kitchen down a hallway. In a darkened room, he set her down on a bed and pulled back. During those few seconds, she felt cold without him.

"Zach?"

"Right here," he said, returning, leaning over her as he opened a foil packet and protected himself. "I don't trust myself much longer."

He slid his hand through her hair and down her face to cup her jaw. "I never thought I'd feel this—" He broke off and shook his head. He trailed his hand down over her breasts and lower, over her abdomen and between her legs where she was hot and moist. "Perfection," he muttered. "All woman."

Toying with her, he took her mouth in a French kiss. The desperation and need tightened inside her so she could hardly stand it. Unable to bear another second, she slid her hand down to where he was hard and big and all male. She stroked down his shaft and he gave a hiss of arousal.

"That's it," he said and pushed her thighs apart. One breath later, he plunged inside her, stretching her, filling her.

He swore. "You feel so good," he said and began to pump. She moved in counterpoint to his sexual invasion, craving every millimeter of him.

She felt the first flush of a climax soar through her. She was so close, so very close, but then he plunged one last time crying out, and sank on top of her.

His weight was heavy, but somehow sweet. His breath flowed over her and she was left with a strange feeling of satisfaction despite the fact that she hadn't gone over the top.

He struggled up to rest on his elbows, looking deep in her gaze, his eyes still dark with sex. "You didn't come," he said.

Surprised, a little self-conscious, she dropped her jaw. "It's not a big deal. Not—"

"I can fix that," he said and lowered his mouth to hers again.

Tina awakened to darkness and a man's heavy leg trapping her lower body. A clock on the bed stand displayed the time as 3:47 a.m. She wasn't sure what had awakened her—perhaps the unfamiliar sensation of sharing a bed with a man who gave satisfaction a completely new and wonderful meaning. Guilt and responsibility that had developed before she exited her mother's womb. Or just the fact that her left leg was falling asleep.

Alarm rushed through her. *What on earth had she done? What on earth was she doing?* Her security detail would be descending on her any minute. She was surprised they hadn't shown up already.

Oh, that wouldn't do, she thought, cringing at the image of Rolfe, her head security man, bursting through the door. *She* had never caused a scandal. *She* was the dependable one. Her brother Stefan, the crown prince, was the one with a temper. Her younger sister was the beautiful, impetuous one with the whole family breathing a sigh of relief that she was settling down. Her other younger siblings were involved with their own lives and personal dramas. Getting them to help with royal duties was like pulling teeth from a wild boar.

Tina was the go-to princess. Someone had to be. She should leave before Zach was dragged into the craziness of her life. Her heart twisted with regret as she studied the hard planes of his face, his dark eyelashes and his dark hair, mussed by her fingertips.

He'd given her a sliver of an out-of-time, out-of-body experience. Thank goodness for these few hours, she thought. She'd never felt more like a woman. Sadness twisted through her as realization sank through. She might never feel like this again.

Sunlight seeped through the blinds of Zach's condominium window. He didn't open his eyes, feeling a bone-deep relaxation and satisfaction that prevented him from any muscle movement. His muscles were relaxed, his mind blessedly blank. For a full moment.

Then flashes of the night before skittered across his brain. His eyes still closed, he saw a woman with sexy, plump lips and inviting eyes and a body that made him hard. Again.

He opened his eyes. *Tina.* He glanced around the bed and inhaled, smelling the scent of her. *Where had she gone?*

"Tina," he called, lifting up on his elbow.

Silence answered him.

"Damn," he muttered and raked his hand through his hair. He shouldn't have brought her here, he thought. She was Keely and Brent's friend. He was supposed to see her safely back to their place.

But she'd been so soft and sexy and irresistible. And now she'd run out on him.

Not until he'd taken her over the edge, he reminded himself. Several times. For both of them. He couldn't remember a wilder night. Not even with his wife.

His gut squeezed at the thought. His dead wife and his dead baby. For a little while, Tina had given him something else to think about. His elbow scraped against something. Metal, he thought, scooping up a small chain. He studied it for a moment, noting the catch had broken. He remembered the way the silver bracelet had played over her skin when she'd caressed him with her hands and mouth.

He closed his eyes, his sense of pleasure and ease evaporating quickly. His little break from pain was over, and his time of torture and self-recrimination had returned.

Twelve hours later, Tina sat in her brother's parlor waiting for his to-do list. He usually delivered it via e-mail, but Tina suspected that since she'd ditched her cell phone for that one night at the masquerade party, he didn't trust electronic communication. Or perhaps he just didn't trust her.

Her brother's assistant had already bowed in greeting a few moments ago. Standing, he waved his hand to the door to Stefan's office. "His Royal Highness will see you now," he said.

Tina could have pushed to eliminate the wait, but after rushed good-byes to her friend Keely, and her transatlantic flight to Chantaine, she was grateful for a moment to catch her breath. "Thank you, Pete," she said and entered her brother's office.

Her brother stood, even though his royal position made it unnecessary, and rounded his large, antique desk. He opened his arms to give her a quick hug. "Welcome home," he said.

"Why is it that we seem to get hit with an onslaught of royal duties every time you leave the country?"

She smiled. "It's the same amount of duties as always. No one picks up the slack."

"I've noticed that," he said with a frown. "Both Bridget and Phillipa have finished their education. They should take on more."

"Good luck with that," she said. "They both have more excuses than there are grains of sand on Senesia Beach," she said, referring to the most popular beach of their island kingdom. "I take it you tried giving them assignments."

"They ignore me," he said, his expression incredulous. "Turn off their cell phones, lose e-mails. If they were staff, they would have been fired ten times over."

Tina laughed. "Tough to fire your sisters."

He shook his head and his mouth drew into a frown. "I'm considering other measures. You've told me again and again about your American friends who believe in earning their way. I can put a limit on their charge cards."

"Ouch," Tina said. "There will be lots of screaming. You may try negotiating first."

"I'm thinking of putting you in charge of them. They need to be trained."

Tina shook her head. "No way. Even Mother didn't train me. A longtime advisor taught me everything. You can bring her out of retirement for the job," she said. *If she doesn't quit.*

Stefan wrinkled his brow. "Something has to be done. With Ericka's upcoming wedding, you'll be busier than ever. I'm focused on plans for the economy and facilitating our diplomatic relationships with countries that can boost our GDP."

"What do the advisers say?

"They recommend that I take a wife. I have no time for courting with my schedule."

"You could always just accept one assigned by the advisers. That's what you wanted me to do," she said, unable to resist the dig. Both her father and brother had urged her to accept an arranged marriage to a man twice her age because he was an Italian count.

"You could have done worse," he said.

"What about Princess Margherita from Italy?" she retorted.

He cringed. "I couldn't bear her laugh for a night let alone for the rest of my life."

"But think of your country, your duty," she began, echoing the same words he'd used with her.

"Enough," he said sharply, lifting his hand.

Tina could tell by the flicker of the tiny muscle in his jaw that she'd pushed a little too far for his comfort. Stefan struggled with his temper, especially when he felt as if things were out of his control.

"The purpose of this meeting is not to discuss your marital prospects or mine," he said. "The purpose is to discuss where you disappeared to for over eight hours last night. Rolfe said he couldn't reach you by cell and that your hostess refused to name your whereabouts when asked."

Tina felt a twist of irritation. "Rolfe is a tattletale."

"He was doing his job," Stefan said. "You know better than this. You must always remain available via your cell. You must always have protection."

"How many times have I been unavailable?" she demanded.

"None to my memory, but that's not the point."

"For that matter, how many times has Ericka been unavailable?"

"Do you really want to be compared to someone who spent

two stints in rehab? Thank God, she's clean now. And who would have thought she would bring a French movie director into the family?" he marveled. "But we count on you to be mature and dependable. You understand your obligations and duties."

"Maybe too much," she whispered to herself, glancing toward the window, feeling more trapped than she'd ever felt in her life. She rubbed her bare wrist, wondering where she'd left her favorite bracelet. She would search through her luggage again for it.

"Valentina," Stefan said in his ruler voice. "Where were you?"

In the past, she would have felt intimidated or at the least, guilty for causing trouble. For some reason, this time she didn't. This time she felt impatient with Stefan's demands.

"I was out," she said, meeting his gaze dead-on.

The muscle in his jaw began to tick again. "These next three months, the eyes of the world will be watching our country in anticipation of Fredericka's wedding. I need you to act with utmost maturity and responsiveness. Ericka will be under enormous pressure now that she's placed in the spotlight. Of all our family, Ericka will trust you."

Tina shook her head. "I can't promise miracles. She needed rehab."

"But even you talked her into that," Stefan said. "I need you to be supportive of her. Keep her together."

"I told you I can't perform miracles."

"Just be your best self," he said. "That's more than almost everyone else on their best day."

She couldn't hold back a semi-smile. "Flattery," she said. "You must be desperate, your highness."

Chapter Three

Zach paced the dentist's office as he waited for his longtime housekeeper to get her broken tooth fixed. Hildie was no wimp. She'd been known to face down two intruders at once with only a frying pan as her weapon. She'd even confronted a brown bear that came a little too close to the house.

Under usual circumstances, Hildie would drive herself to the doctor if she were sick. Hildie had helped deliver babies. She wasn't squeamish at all. Dentists, however, were her waterloo. She'd procrastinated going to the dentist and now the poor woman winced every time she breathed.

Zach had insisted she go in and Hildie agreed only if he would take her and wait for her. They never knew which sedation the dentist would use. It was all determined by Hildie's anxiety level, which today, hovered at one hundred on a scale of one to ten.

Bored, Zach sank onto one of the chairs and checked his BlackBerry. His brother wanted him to cover for him in

Dallas while he took a scuba diving trip. No problem. Zach was always around. It wasn't as if anything exciting was going on in his life, and he preferred it that way. Particularly in his personal life.

He couldn't deny, at least to himself, though, that ever since that night with Tina, he'd almost asked his friends how to get in touch with her. Every time he was tempted, however, he remembered the tragic ending of his marriage.

No. He wasn't ready to have a woman in his life. He didn't know if he would ever be ready. Restlessness nicked at his nerve endings and he rolled his neck to release some tension. Desperate to distract himself, he picked up the trashy gossip rag on the table and skimmed the front page.

The theme of the day seemed to be babies. He felt his gut clench at the memory of the loss of his own child, but shook the paper and kept reading. Senator's love child living in an igloo in Alaska. Movie stars adopt three more children. Dog helps deliver baby. Pregnant Princess? Who's your daddy?

He almost tossed it back onto the cheap table holding the rest of women's magazines. But as he flipped through the pages in disgust, an image of something he'd seen before flashed before him. A young curvy woman with brown hair. In the photo, she wore a hat and a loose-fitting dress. Her belly was amplified in a photo insert.

Zach frowned at the photo and quickly read the article. *Princess Valentina of Chantaine has stood by the side of her fragile sister bride nonstop during the huge wedding that drew the focus of the entire world. Tina has always been the good girl in the royal family, but maybe she isn't so perfect after all. Has Tina gained a little weight? Strange that her weight gain isn't all over…just in her belly. Insiders report Princess Tina fought nausea throughout the wedding festivities. If the princess is pregnant, where is the baby daddy?*

Or did she give up on her prospects and enlist the services of a sperm bank? Time will tell.

Princess, Zach thought. What the— *Princess Tina*. She hadn't mentioned being a princess. What kind of job had she said she had? Something in international relations.

He gave a cynical laugh. Cute, he thought. Real cute. He wondered how in hell Keely was friends with a princess.

Glancing at the slight baby bump, he felt a tight knot form in his chest. She couldn't be pregnant, he thought. He'd used protection. He mentally flipped through the night they'd spent together. Every time they'd made love. And they'd made love a lot. Had there been one time when he'd forgotten or been too eager to feel her close around him or—

He had a vivid memory of feeling her wet velvet with no barrier.

"Damn," he muttered, pulling off his hat. Was she pregnant? If so, that baby could be his.

Panic ripped through him. His heart raced, skipping and sinking. A horrible dread tugged at him, sinking to his gut and lower, dragging him down. He swore at himself ten times over. What had he been thinking?

He hadn't been thinking. He'd been feeling. That was the problem. Feeling always caused problems.

Sucking in a long breath, he stared at her photo and that damned baby bump insert. He would find out if she was pregnant and he would find out if the baby was his. He clenched his fist in determination. It wouldn't take him long.

For once, Tina's sister came through for her. It was a huge switch. Although Ericka was happily busy and traveling hither and yon with her new husband, she said Tina could stay at her new home just outside of Paris. Close enough to the city, but far enough from the congestion, the new home was perfect for the respite Tina needed.

Tina had escaped just as her brother began to insist she was due for an examination from the royal doctors. Before her plane landed in Paris, rumors in the gossip rags had exploded. She'd only been away for twenty-four hours and her voice mail box was full. She didn't even want to look at her e-mail.

She knew her brother was going to freak out, and her security man, Rolfe, was watching her every move. Thank goodness she and her sister had worked out a plan for this very situation. An older woman, Genieve, brought fresh vegetables most every morning and brought pastry treats for the staff. She usually left from the back entrance of the house around noon. Except today. Today Genieve would stay until 4:00 p.m. and watch television with one of the favorite staff members in a room upstairs while Tina dressed in dark clothes with a dark scarf covering her head and drove the woman's car to a small, out-of-the-way museum with beautiful gardens.

There, Tina could think about her and her baby's future. There, she could make plans.

Tina told Rolfe she planned to take a nap and didn't want to be disturbed. As soon as he left her hallway, she took the back stairs to the back entrance and got into the ancient vehicle and escaped.

The July heat was oppressive, but the temperature inside the small museum was cool. She noticed only a few tourists, but an abundance of caution made her keep her head covered. Glancing outside, she saw no one in the gardens and walked outside to a stone bench beside a small pond. Despite the shade from the tree, the heat forced her to pull off her scarf.

She closed her eyes, craving peace and quiet for her mind and soul. She didn't need panic in this situation. She needed to remain calm. Since everyone else was going to be emotionally jumping out of windows.

Tina could see the headlines now. *Unwed Pregnant Princess.* She, the one everyone counted on to be scandal-free. She laughed softly to herself, although she still struggled with a twinge of hysteria. Was she prepared to be a single mother? It didn't matter. That's what she would be. She stroked her abdomen, feeling protective of the baby growing there.

Tina had always put her loyalty to her position first, but there was no doubt in her mind what was most important to her now. Her child. Her pregnancy might be unexpected, unplanned and her situation not exactly optimal, but that didn't change the fact that Tina would make her child her priority.

That solid knowledge released a tension from inside her. She took a deep breath and gave into the temptation to build a perfect little world for her and her baby in her mind. The two of them could live here in France, near her sister. She would lead a simple life raising her child, serving as a patron for her favorite charities and making rare appearances in Chantaine.

Her sisters would pitch in and take over her assignments. *That was pure fantasy,* she thought. And her brother would marry a woman who would keep him out of her hair. *More fantasy.*

She inhaled again, lingering over the idyllic image in her mind.

Something fell beside her on the bench. *A chain?* She opened her eyes and glanced beside her, immediately spotting the bracelet she'd thought she'd lost.

"Been missing that?" a deep male voice that had haunted her dreams said to her.

She glanced behind her, directly into the hard blue gaze of Zachary Logan. Her heart stopped in her chest. Her breath froze in her lungs.

"The baby's mine, isn't it?"

* * *

Zach didn't like her color. She'd gone past the pale stage and she looked gray. He handed her his bottle of water. "Here, you look like you need this."

She stared at him without blinking, seemingly without breathing for another long moment. "Tina," he said and squeezed her shoulder. "Drink some water."

At his touch, she finally took a breath and looked away. "I didn't think I would ever see you again," she said. "How did you find me?"

"A combination of Keely and a private investigator. I've had a guy watching your sister's house for every person who came and went. I tried calling your assistant, but she blew me off."

She looked up at him in alarm. "Did you tell her you and I had—"

"No, but I was tempted," he said, reining in his frustration from the last several days. "When were you going to tell me about the baby?"

Tina blinked. "I—I wasn't," she said with a shrug.

Shock rushed through him. "You what?" he nearly shouted.

Tina glanced around in alarm. "Please keep your voice down. I don't want to draw attention. I came here to think."

Zach's stomach turned. "Are you saying you're not keeping the baby?"

She looked at him in confusion. "What do you mean? Give the baby up for adoption—"

"No, I meant," he said and stopped, his throat closing over his words. "I meant end the pregnancy."

Shock widened her eyes. "Absolutely not."

Some small something inside him eased and he took a quick breath. "That still doesn't explain why you weren't going to tell me."

She gave a sigh of frustration. "It was a one-night stand. It didn't seem fair to drag you into it."

"It's my child too," he said in a deadly firm voice.

"Yes, but it's not just about the baby," she said and lifted her hands. "Dealing with who I am, who my family is, what's expected of me and my family. Not many men can handle that. You don't really even know me. It's not as if we're in love. Being involved with the baby and me would turn your life upside down."

"You don't think it already has?"

Her lips parted in surprise, as if she had truly believed he wouldn't be interested in his own child. "I'm sorry," she said softly. "I shouldn't have rushed to the assumption that you would only view this as a burden."

"There's a difference between burden and responsibility," he said.

She nodded. "That's very true. I'm just not accustomed to dealing with men who know how to distinguish the two."

"Maybe you've been hanging around the wrong men," he said.

Her lips lifted in amusement. "Maybe so."

"Do you know what your plans are?" he asked. "Are you going to live in your country?"

Tina looked down at her hands folded in her lap and shook her head. "My brother is going to freak out. He might have expected something like this from my younger sister, but never me. I know he's in a difficult situation, but I just wish I could go away for a while. I need to get my head on straight about all this and doing that in Chantaine is going to be very, very difficult, if not impossible."

"I have the perfect place if you need to think. My ranch," he said.

She blinked at the recommendation. "Your ranch?" she echoed as if that possibility was last on her list.

"Sure," he said with a shrug. "It's no palace, but most people who visit like it. It's quiet. You would be able to think. Plus," he said, "it would give you an opportunity to get to know the father of your child better."

She met his gaze and a glimmer of the night they'd shared seemed to pass through her eyes. Licking her lips, she glanced away. Zach felt a surprising bolt of sexual awareness stab at him. *Where the hell had that come from?*

"What do you say?" he asked.

"I don't know," she said. "I hadn't even considered this until this moment. I can't make an instant decision."

"Why not?" he asked. "You have a passport. You're an adult. You can do whatever you think is best for you and your child."

At that moment, a group of men with cameras and microphones burst into the garden. "Princess Valentina, tell us the truth. Are you pregnant?"

"Oh, no." Tina stood and backed away.

Zach automatically stepped in front of her. "Leave her alone," he said.

"Who are you?" the short, portly reporter continued. "You're not her regular bodyguard. Are you her lover?" he asked. "The father of her child?"

Cameras snapped and the reporter pressed against him. "Leave us alone. Get out of here."

The reporter continued to push against Zach, irritating him with his persistence. "You sound American. What's your name?"

"None of your damn business," Zach said. "Step aside. You're bothering Tina."

The reporter pushed past Zach and began to crowd Tina. "Tina," the reporter echoed. "Who is this man? How far along are you? Are you getting married?"

Zach pushed his way between the reporter and Tina. "Last warning. Step aside."

The reporter ignored him and Zach knocked him to the ground. He picked up Tina and carried her out of the garden.

Tina gawked at Zach. "What are you doing?"

"Getting you the hell away from those wackos," he said, heedless of the stares he drew as he hauled her through the small museum.

"Where are we going?" she asked as he tucked her into a rental car and got into the driver's seat. He started the engine and put the car into gear.

He glanced at her. "Where do you want to go?"

Her heart dipped at his expression. Her heart, in fact, hadn't beat regularly since she'd looked up to see him in the museum courtyard.

"Do you want to go back to your sister's house?" he asked.

Her stomach twisted. "Not really. My bodyguard will insist that I talk to my brother. He may even push me into going back to Chantaine."

Zach made a U-turn. "Okay, that's out. We could go to my hotel."

"So public," she said. "If you think the paparazzi was bad here…"

He shrugged. "Okay. How about my ranch?"

She gulped, taking in the way his large hand shifted gears. "That would require a flight. That could take some time."

Zach shifted gears and accelerated. He met her gaze. "Not necessarily. I can have a jet ready in an hour."

Surprise raced through her. "That would be expensive," she said, aware of the cost of private transatlantic flights because she usually flew first-class to save the royal family some change.

"I can handle it," he said with a shrug of his powerful shoulders. "I usually fly first-class for the legroom, but the jet's always at my disposal. But are you sure about this?"

Tina felt another forbidden thrill. Her brother would wring her neck. Her sisters would curse her for leaving them to deal with her brother. She bit the inside of her lip and nodded. "I'm sure."

Chapter Four

Half a day later, Tina awakened to the sensation of Zach's jet landing on a runway. Rousing herself from her slumber, she squinted out the window to see the flat landscape surrounding the Dallas Fort Worth International Airport.

She glanced across the aisle at Zach. He was looking outside the window on his side of the jet. His long lean legs extended before him, his dark hair was mussed. She wondered if he had slept half as much as she had.

She realized again that she had committed to going to his ranch. He was a man she knew intimately. In most ways, however, she barely knew him at all, and he barely knew her.

A knot of nerves formed in her throat. What in the world had she done? Tina took a deep breath. *Give yourself a break. You didn't have a lot of choices.*

Zach turned to look at her. "We're here. I can get a helicopter. Otherwise it's an hour and a half drive to my ranch."

"There's no need for a helicopter," she said. "I've slept most of the flight. A car will be fine."

"You're sure?" he asked.

She nodded, smiling. "I'm sure."

His gaze did things to her. She looked away to gather her things. He ushered her out of the plane and down the steps to the tarmac.

Two armed officers immediately approached them. "Mr. Logan, we need to question you about the kidnapping of Valentina Devereaux."

Zach blinked. "Excuse me?" he said.

"Oh, no," Tina whispered. "This is either my brother or my security guard. Or both." Refusing to be a victim, refusing to allow Zach to be a victim, she went into Princess-mode. "Pardon me, officer, but there's obviously been a misunderstanding. Mr. Logan graciously allowed me to be a passenger on his jet. I was being pursued by the paparazzi and he provided me with a safe escape."

The uniformed men exchanged glances. "His Majesty, Stefan Devereaux, insists you were taken against your will."

"His Majesty is mistaken," she said, lifting her chin. "I am here and this is where I wish to be."

"Give me a minute," one of the officers said.

The two men exchanged an extensive whispered conversation, then turned toward her. One pulled out a cell phone. "Clear it with His Majesty. I don't want a diplomatic incident on my head," the man said with a southern drawl.

"Clear it," she echoed, unable to keep the indignation from her voice. "I'm an adult. I don't have to clear this with any—"

"Tina, make the call or I'll be here all night," Zach said.

Giving a heavy sigh, she took the officer's phone, stabbed out her brother's personal cell number and waited. One ring. Two rings. *He damn well better pick up,* she thought.

"Stefan," the male voice finally announced. Two seconds later, he swore. "What the hell are you doing, Valentina?"

"I'm visiting Texas by my own free will," she said. "I sent both you and Rolfe a text message explaining my plans."

"The paparazzi said you were carried out of a museum by a madman," Stefan said.

"He was protecting me," she said.

"Humph," Stefan said, disbelief oozing through his voice. "Who is this Zachary Logan?"

She paused a half beat, then decided to break the news. "He's the father of my baby."

Silence followed. "So it's true," Stefan said, his voice turning hard. "Tina, how could you?"

She bit her lip at the disapproval in his voice. "The usual way," she said.

Stefan let out a litany of oaths.

She narrowed her eyes and interjected. "I'm putting you on speaker phone for the armed officers so there won't be a need for Zachary Logan to be detained."

The litany abruptly stopped.

"So, Stefan, we now agree that there has been a terrible misunderstanding and I have not been kidnapped. Correct?"

"Correct," he said in a clipped voice.

"And just for the benefit of the kind officers, please state your name," she said.

"Tina," he said, with a warning note in his voice.

"You're the one who pushed the kidnapping charges," she said.

Stefan cleared his throat. "Stefan Edward Henri Jacques the fifth."

"Thank you, Stefan," she said and he hung up. "Good luck," she whispered, thinking of her sweet, but spoiled sisters.

Zach glanced down at her. "Ready to go?"

"You have no idea," she said.

He slid his hand behind her back and steered her toward the private terminal. "I've heard of overprotective older brothers, but—"

"He's terrified of losing me. My sisters are useless." She felt a stab of guilt. "By choice. They would be terrific if they would think about anyone but themselves."

"Isn't that true of half the world?" he drawled.

"Yes," she said, smiling. "I guess it is. I apologize about the near-arrest."

"Something tells me that won't be the last excitement I see as a result of having you around," he said.

Tina winced. "I warned you."

"Yeah," he said. "You did. Let's get out of here."

Zach ushered her into the same SUV he'd driven all those months ago when he'd taken her to his apartment. She inhaled the scent, feeling a flood of sensual memories skitter through her.

She sank into the leather seat, feeling safe and for the first time in months, not judged. Closing her eyes, she tried to make sense of her most recent, most impulsive decision of her life.

"I don't have any clothes," she said.

"No problem," he said. "You can sleep in one of my T-shirts and go shopping tomorrow or the next day."

"Your T-shirt," she echoed, finding the prospect incredibly sensual and forbidden.

"Yeah," he said. "Unless her highness requires silk."

She paused a half-beat and decided to push back a little. She suspected she'd been way too easy for him. That put her at a disadvantage. "Silk? I can skip a night."

He gave a low laugh that rippled along her nerve endings.

"Tell me something I don't know," he said. "You skipped every stitch of clothing the night you spent with me."

"I'm surprised you remember," she said. "It was just one night—"

He whipped his head around to meet her gaze. "I remember everything about that night, Tina. Everything."

Just as Zach had said, ninety minutes later, he pulled down a long driveway lined with scrubby landscape. "Is this it?" she asked, preparing herself for a log cabin.

He nodded and she noticed the dirt and scrub were replaced by green grass and trees. "Is this your family home, or did you acquire it?"

"It's been in my family for generations. Some of the staff live in the original homeplace. I had a new home built about six years ago," he said.

A large white building with a wraparound front porch sat amidst tall trees and flowering shrubs. The waning sunlight glistened on the leaves. "It's beautiful," she said.

He glanced at her. "You sound surprised."

"I didn't know what to expect. A ranch can mean different things to different people."

"Ah, so you were expecting something more primitive. I hope you're not disappointed," he joked.

"Not at all," she said, looking forward to a shower.

"If I know Hildie, she'll have a meal waiting for us when we walk in the door," he said.

"Hildie?"

"Cook and housekeeper. She's been working at the ranch since before my parents passed away," he said.

"It's nice to have that continuity. We have a few staff members and advisers who have been around a long time."

"Are you worried about getting homesick? This is a lot different than Chantaine."

"I'm counting on that," she said with a sigh. More than anything, Tina craved an opportunity to hear herself think.

Zach pulled the SUV to a stop, then got out and stepped to the passenger door to open her door. He extended his hand and she took it, remembering the sensation of his calloused palms on various places of her body. Leading her up the steps, he opened the door and she stepped into a terra cotta tiled double-story foyer that featured a double staircase. A copper and crystal chandelier hung from the ceiling.

The foyer was warm and welcoming without being pretentious. She felt a sliver of tension ease from inside her. She took a short breath and inhaled the scent of a mouthwatering meal.

"Zach, is that you?" a woman called. Seconds later, a tall, sturdy woman with iron gray hair and a stern face entered the foyer. Her mouth softened slightly, but she still didn't quite smile. "There you are. The phone's been ringing off the hook. Some kook named Rolfe got all snippy with me, accusing you of kidnapping. I finally just hung up on the man."

Tina cringed. She generally tried to avoid creating drama, but this time she hadn't seen any other way around it.

"Yeah, well, I think we took care of that," Zach said, shooting Tina a sideways glance. "This is Valentina Devereaux, Hildie." He cleared his throat. "Princess Valentina Devereaux."

Hildie's eyes widened in surprise. "Princess?" she echoed. "You didn't really kidnap a princess, did you?" She glanced at Tina. "I mean, I know it's been awhile since you've been on a date, but—"

"Hildie," Zach interjected. "Tina is pregnant with my child."

Hildie's jaw dropped. "When in tarnation did that happen?"

Tina felt her cheeks heat at Hildie's suspicious expression. "It wasn't planned, Miss—?"

"Just Hildie. Everybody calls me Hildie. And what do I call you? Your majesty? Your highlyness."

"Tina would be fine," she said.

"Humph," Hildie said and lifted an eyebrow at Zach. "You said you were bringing a guest, not a princess. She may not like beef stew."

"I'm sure it's wonderful," Tina rushed to say. "I'll try not to be any trouble. I'm just looking forward to the quiet."

"Well, we've got a lot of that around here. Come on in. Dinner's waiting," Hildie said and walked down the hall.

"Oh, dear," Tina said. "I believe I've already upset her."

"Don't worry," Zach said, putting his hand on her lower back and guiding her farther into the house. "Hildie may look like she's just taken a bite out of a green apple, but she's got a heart of gold."

Hildie served the hearty meal in the kitchen nook instead of the formal dining room. Zach was pleased to see Tina eat a healthy portion of the stew and corn bread, although he didn't eat as much as usual. Although he'd been determined to bring Tina home, now that she was here, he was on edge. The ranch had become his cave, the place where he could hide and grieve. He hadn't brought a woman to the ranch since his wife had died.

Hildie refilled the water glasses. "So when's the wedding?"

Tina choked on a bite of her corn bread. "Oh no," she said, taking a long drink of water. "No wedding. Zach and I barely know each other."

"Well, you know each other well enough to get preg—"

"Hildie," Zach interjected. "Tina just arrived here. She just made the decision to come to the ranch yesterday. Let her settle in."

"Humph," Hildie said. "It don't make sense to me."

Hildie left the room and Tina leaned toward him. "Is she always this opinionated?"

He nodded. "And she doesn't hold back. Don't worry. She'll adjust. If she gets too pushy, just tell her to back off."

Tina bit her lip. "I can't fathom telling that woman to back off."

"Pretend she's your brother," he said.

Her lips lifted in a smile and he felt something in his gut twist. The sensation took him by surprise. "If you're done, I'll show you around the house."

"Thank you. That would be nice," she said and followed him to her feet as he rose.

Zach led her through the den, formal areas and his office area downstairs, then took her upstairs. Proud of the home he'd designed and helped build several years ago, he couldn't help wondering what Tina thought of it. She paused at the collection of family photographs in the upstairs hallway. "Is this your mother and father?" she asked. "And these other children? I think I remember you mentioning a brother."

He nodded. "Yeah, those are my parents, and my brother and sister," he said, pointing to another photograph. He felt a twinge of regret. His relationship with his brother and sister had suffered after the death of his wife. He'd shut everyone out.

Surprised at the onslaught of emotions he was experiencing, he cleared his throat. "Your room is down the hall," he said and walked toward the largest of the guest rooms. His former wife had chosen the colors for this room. Shades of green and blue-green provided a soothing haven. His own blood pressure always seemed to drop a few notches when he stepped into this room.

"Oh, it's lovely," Tina said. "I love the colors."

"Good," he said with a nod. "There's a connecting bath

with plenty of towels. I'll bring a couple of shirts for you. The remote for the TV should be on the nightstand. Anything else you need that you can think of?"

"Toothbrush and toothpaste," she said.

"I'll tell Hildie to bring you some. Anything else?" he asked, feeling his heart tug at the vulnerable expression on her face. Giving into an urge, he extended his hand to her arm and gently squeezed. "You're safe here," he said. "I'll make sure of it."

She took a deep breath and appeared to stiffen her spine. "Thank you. I'm afraid of how much I'm imposing."

"You're the mother of my child," he said firmly. "This is no imposition. You've been taking care of everyone else. It's damn time someone looked after you."

She blinked. "I have royal doctors and assistants. I didn't mean to give you the impression that I have to do everything on my own because I don't."

"Maybe," he said. "But it's pretty clear your family doesn't put your health or your need to take a break first. Now that you're pregnant, that needs to change. I can make sure that will happen."

"What about the paparazzi? They always show up," she said, her eyes darkening with fear.

"I have electric fences and gates. I don't usually have to close those gates, but I can and I will. Plus there's Hildie. She took on a brown bear one time. The bear turned tail and ran."

Tina stared at him for a long moment, then laughed. "Oh, my goodness, I can easily visualize that."

The sound of her laughter eased something inside him. He smiled. "I'm not stretching the truth. The only thing that scares Hildie is the dentist. I had to take her to fix a broken tooth. That's how I found out you were pregnant."

Tina lifted her hand to her throat. "At the dentist's office?"

"I was in the waiting room killing time. I saw your photo in one of those gossip sheets."

She winced. "The bump article," she said. "I received an anonymous tip from someone that the article was going to be published and left Chantaine just before the story hit. I was hoping to avoid the first wave from the media while I figured out how to handle everything."

"France wasn't far enough," he said.

"Nowhere is far enough," she said woefully. "I'm afraid you don't know what you've gotten yourself into by bringing me to your home."

"I've been through worse," he said, his own personal tragedy never far from his mind.

She widened her eyes. "With the media?"

He shrugged. "With life," he said. "Don't worry about me. The media is the least of my concern. Get some rest. If you need anything, let Hildie or me know. I'll let her take you into town so you can get what you need tomorrow."

She still looked vulnerable. His hands ached to pull her against him, but he resisted the urge. She wasn't exactly the same woman who had gone to bed with him months ago. Back then, he hadn't known she was a princess. Back then, she hadn't wanted him to know. She'd wanted one anonymous night just as he had. Now, everything was different. In a way, they were strangers more now than ever before.

She licked her lips and a flash of that dark night of need snapped through him. "Thank you for taking me away. For bringing me here."

Zach gave into the urge to stroke her hair and cup her head. "I know you're still wound tighter than a spring, but you're safe here. Soon enough, you'll realize you can relax.

And no thanks are necessary. I wouldn't have it any other way. 'Night Tina."

She took a deep breath that seemed to tremble out of her when she exhaled. "Good night, Zach."

Chapter Five

When Tina awakened the next morning, the sun slithered through the curtains covering the windows. She heard a vague vibrating sound, but couldn't quite place it. Glancing at one side of the bed then the other, she squinted at the clock on the nightstand. 10:30 a.m.

Embarrassment rolled through her. Oh, my Lord. She'd slept for twelve hours. Everyone would think she was the clichéd princess, accustomed to rising late, when that couldn't be further from the truth. The soft buzzing sound continued and she finally placed the noise. Her cell phone. Blinking, she pushed her hair from her face and slid out of bed. Where had she put the darn thing?

Following the sound, she finally found it beneath her discarded clothes from the night before. At the moment, she wore one of Zach's T-shirts and the well-worn cotton felt delicious against her skin. She pulled out her cell phone and surveyed the recent calls. Her brother, her sister in Paris, her next youngest sister, her assistant, her brother, her brother, and her sister in Paris.

Sighing, she mentally formed a strategy for each call and pushed speed dial for her brother.

"How long are you planning on staying there?" her brother demanded as he picked up the phone.

"I'm not going to have a long discussion. As I told you before, I'm here in Texas of my own free will. Not sure when I'll return. I'm figuring things out."

"Figuring things out?" her brother echoed. "And how are we supposed to deal with this? I'm shocked at your lack of consideration."

"Consider it belated rebellion," she said. "I'll be in touch when I can give you more information."

"But Tina, how are we to explain this to the press?"

"I don't really care," she said. "You have professionals on staff to take care of this. Let them do their job."

"And what about your appearances?"

"Either cancel them or let my sisters step up. Take care, sweetie," she said and disconnected the call.

She called her sister in Paris to reassure her that she hadn't been abducted. Ericka was shocked that Tina was pregnant out of wedlock, but recovered enough to offer Tina any and every assistance.

"How could you do this to me? I've only been out of college for two years and just when I'm enjoying life in Florence, Stefan insists I move back to Chantaine?" her younger sister, Bridget, said when Tina called.

"That's two more years than I had," Tina said, more blunt than she'd ever been with her younger sister.

"But this is a terrible scandal," Bridget said. "There will be questions every which way I turn. How will I answer them?"

"That's what the palace PR is for. They will help you,"

Tina said, feeling the urge to return to bed and pull the covers over her head.

"But Tina, how could you do this? Everyone was counting on you to be the normal one," her sister huffed.

Tina sighed. "Maybe that's why it happened. I just couldn't be normal and dutiful anymore. I'm sorry. I—" Her voice broke and she swallowed over the lump in her throat. "You'll do fine. Maybe better than me," she said. "Love you. Bye for now."

She disconnected the call and turned off the phone. She couldn't bear hearing the disappointment in her family's voices one more minute. Her eyes burned with unshed tears and she tried to hold them back, but they seemed to well up from her belly to her tight chest and tighter throat. A sob escaped and then another. Tears streamed down her cheeks. She couldn't remember the last time she'd cried like this. When her mother had died? When her father had passed away?

A sharp rap sounded on the bedroom door, startling her. She sniffed and swiped at her wet cheeks.

"Hildie here. I have breakfast for you," the housekeeper said and opened the door.

Horrified, Tina groped for something to cover herself. In her world, staff never entered without receiving confirmation from her.

Hildie bustled around the room. "I don't often get a chance to deliver breakfast in bed, but since you're here I do. Lord knows, Zachary never sleeps past dawn," she said with more than a twinge of disapproval as she placed the tray on a table. "It's a good thing you rested well, being pregnant and all. I read that it takes a day to adjust to each time zone change, so you've got a few days to go. And according to what Zachary said, they've been running you like a mule during harvest. A woman with child needs her rest. I hope some of this will suit you. Scrambled eggs, bacon, pancakes, grits, fruit and toast."

Hildie finally glanced at Tina. The woman narrowed her gaze as she studied her then caught sight of the phone in Tina's hand. "You've been crying. Has someone been bothering you?"

Tina sniffled but shook her head. "Not bothering. I had to return a few calls."

"To who?" Hildie asked crossing her arms over her chest.

"Just a few members of my family," Tina said, wondering why she felt the need to answer questions from staff.

"Humph," Hildie said. "Well, if they're upsetting you, it just won't do. Zachary won't allow it."

Taken off guard by the woman's suggestion that Zachary would somehow be able to control or even influence her family, she shook her head. "Excuse me? Zachary won't allow it? My family doesn't operate by everyone else's rules."

"Neither does Zachary Logan," Hildie said flatly. "But I imagine since he got you out of France in no time flat, you got a taste of what he's capable of. If not, you'll see soon enough. Go ahead and eat. Zachary tells me you need to go to the store. It takes about a half hour to drive to town and I suspect you'll tire quickly."

"I'm really not that fragile," Tina insisted, moving to the table where Hildie had placed her breakfast.

"Uh-huh," Hildie said. "That's what a lot of moms-to-be say. Then all of a sudden they're passing out or crying because they haven't had enough rest."

Offended, Tina lifted her chin. "I wasn't crying because I hadn't had enough—"

"With all due respect, Miss Highlyness," Hildie interjected. "Please eat your breakfast. We're wasting daylight."

Thirty minutes later, Tina joined Hildie in a black Ford

truck. Tina was clean, but her face was stripped clean of cosmetics except for lip gloss and a little powder. Her hair was still damp as Hildie barreled down the road.

Tina gripped the door with one hand and the edge of her seat with the other. "Are we in a hurry?" she asked.

Hildie shrugged and turned the country radio station to a higher decibel. "Not really. I just don't like to waste time getting where I want to go."

Tina swallowed over a knot of panic in her throat. "How far to the store?"

Hildie waved her hand and guided the steering wheel with her knee. "Not long," she said and cackled. "You can be sure I'll get there in no time."

If we don't meet our maker first, she thought and continued her death grip. Hildie gave a running commentary on the history of the area and talked about her niece, Eve, apparently her pride and joy.

When Hildie pulled into a parking lot and screeched to a stop, Tina breathed a sigh of relief.

"Here we are," Hildie said and winked at her. "They have a maternity department here."

Tina walked into the store and felt as if she'd stepped into a foreign country. The truth was that her assistant often shopped for her. Tina rarely visited retail stores. She was too busy.

She felt Hildie studying her. "What's wrong?" she asked. "Don't they have what you want?"

"They seem to have everything. I just don't know where to start. I'm overwhelmed," she said.

Hildie laughed. "Okay, let's start with the basics, then. Underwear," she said and led her to the intimates department.

Tina chose several pairs of stretchy panties and a couple bras.

"You'll get bigger there, too," Hildie warned.

Feeling self-conscious, Tina shrugged. "I'll deal with that later. I'd like to get a couple of skirts and a few tops."

"The maternity department is over—"

"I'm not quite ready for that," Tina said. "I'll just buy a size larger than usual."

"If you're sure," Hildie said.

"I'm not that big yet," Tina whispered. "I'm not that far along in my pregnancy. I'm not ready for everyone to know—"

"Your Highlyness, if Zach noticed your baby bump in that newspaper, then everyone knows," Hildie said dryly.

"Everyone doesn't know at first sight, though. I could just use a little breathing room," Tina said.

Hildie studied her for a long moment. "I can understand that. Let's find you a nice little skirt or two."

Less than fifteen minutes later, they left the store with toiletries, underwear, two skirts, three tops and a dress.

"You won't be able to hide it much longer, dear," Hildie said.

Tina's stomach knotted. "I know. I'm just buying a little time."

"Are you ashamed?" Hildie asked.

"Well, you have to admit it's not the optimal situation," Tina said, gazing out the window as they whizzed past the barren landscape.

"Are you ashamed of Zach?"

Tina whipped her head around to look at Hildie. "No. I'm embarrassed because I should have been more careful, more responsible. It's not as if I were a teenager."

"From what Zachary told me, you were busy being an adult when you were a teenager. No time for impulsiveness or getting into trouble."

"That still doesn't excuse—"

"Pardon me, Your Highlyness, but nobody's perfect. Even

princesses aren't perfect. You're just lucky Zachary was the man who got carried away with you. He's a good man," she said. "And it's time he got past…" Hildie's voice trailed off and she sighed.

"Got past what?" Tina asked.

Hildie frowned. "It's not my place to say."

Tina blinked, shocked that Hildie would consider any subject outside propriety. After all, Zach's housekeeper had freely given her opinions on underwear, pregnancy and marriage. What subject could possibly be so forbidden with Zach?

Glancing at Hildie's implacable expression, she felt a strange sense of forboding. What did she really know about Zachary Logan? Had she made a mistake by coming here?

For the next two days, Tina didn't see Zach. Although she appreciated the opportunity for extra rest and quiet time, she felt frustrated about the lack of opportunity to get to know him better. After all, wasn't that part of the reason she'd come to his ranch?

Donning tennis shoes her sister had included in a package she'd sent her, along with a loose pair of jeans and blouse, she decided to go for a walk. The heat and humidity were already intense, even at nine thirty. Tina wished she'd risen early but knew she was still adjusting to the change in time zones. Pregnancy exacerbated her jet lag, but she felt herself getting stronger.

Spotting a barn with a fenced pasture and a couple of horses, she walked toward it. When she was a teenager, Tina had loved horseback riding. Unfortunately she'd had little time for it once she'd left for college.

She walked into the cool barn and peeked into the stalls. Two quarter horses roomed next to each other, then a gorgeous palomino and black gelding. She wandered toward the pasture and saw a tall, slim, dark-haired woman talking to a colt. The young horse's ears twitched.

Curious, Tina continued to watch in silence.

The woman must have felt her presence, however, because she turned to look at her. "Hello, I'm working with Samson right now. There's no other riding."

Surprised and impressed at the woman's assertiveness, Tina shook her head. "I wasn't planning to ride," she said. "I'm a guest of Mr. Logan's and I was just taking a walk. Pardon me, I didn't mean to intrude."

The woman nodded. "No problem. You can watch if you like. This colt of Zach's is a little ornery, so I'm working with him."

Tina watched as the woman led the colt in a series of walking and stopping around the corral. Constantly cooing, she put a saddle on the colt. He gave a half-beat of a pause then allowed her to lead him again around the corral.

She gave the young horse an apple and praised him effusively then returned him to his stall, which was waiting with fresh oats and water.

Finally, she turned to Tina. "I'm Eve, Hildie's niece," she said.

Tina nodded and extended her hand. "I'm Tina. Hildie has talked about you. She's so proud of you," she said.

Eve nodded, giving a self-conscious smile as she shook Tina's hand. "Hildie's wonderful, but she's a little over the top sometimes."

"In your case, it's over the top in a good way," Tina said.

"Ah," Eve said. "You've obviously spent enough time with her to understand her."

"It didn't take long. She definitely speaks her mind," Tina said.

Eve laughed. "That's an understatement. How do you know Zach?"

"Mutual friends," she said. "I met him several months ago. I could have sworn Hildie told me that you worked for an international hotel chain as a regional manager."

"That's right," Eve said. "This is my fun time. My day off. I used to do more training and Zach made me promise that I would always come back in case he had any problems. Samson here is a problem."

"How did he wrangle that agreement out of you?"

"Paid for all my education that wasn't covered by scholarships," she said then shrugged. "But I don't mind. I really do enjoy my time with horses. They're lots more fun than corporate meetings." She glanced over her back at the stalls. "I should have asked after I finished with Samson. Do you ride? Would you like to ride today? Candy's a nice ride—"

"No, that's okay," Tina said. "I ride, but it's been a while…."

"She's not riding," Zach said from the other end of the barn.

Her heart jumping in her chest, Tina whipped her head around to stare at him. He wore jeans, a T-shirt, a hat, a pair of boots and a frown.

"I wasn't planning on riding," Tina said defensively. "I was just exploring."

"Just don't get into trouble," he said.

Tina frowned. "What kind of trouble? I'm just walking around *your* ranch. I can't stay cooped up in the house forever."

"I guess not," he said as he moved toward her. "Hildie told me you went for a walk."

"Why doesn't that surprise me?" Tina murmured.

"And a good morning to you," Eve said. "Samson's making progress."

Zach nodded. "Good to know," he said. "I hope he hasn't been too much of a pain in the butt."

"No more than his owner," Eve said.

Zach shot her a withering glance. "Anyone ever tell you that you look like your aunt?"

"Bite me," Eve said and turned her back to him.

"How's the job going?" he asked.

"It's going," she said. "I don't love it. I don't hate it."

"Just haven't found what you're looking for," he said.

"It pays well," she said over her shoulder. "That's good enough for me. And, hey, don't be so hard on your visitor. She's polite, which is more than you can say about yourself." She stomped out of the barn.

Feeling Zach's gaze on her, Tina wondered about the relationship between Zach and Eve. Antagonistic, yet vaguely caring.

"Don't even think about riding a horse," he said.

"I didn't," she said. "In more than a fictional sense," she added, seeing a flash of alarm on his face. "When I walked into the barn, I remembered how much I enjoyed riding. How much I missed it, but now isn't the time to—"

"Exactly," he said in a crisp tone. "Now is not the time to start this particular hobby again. It's too dangerous for you and the baby."

She saw a darkness deepen in his eyes and wondered where that originated. She thought about what Hildie had said to her. She thought about how much she didn't know about him.

Lifting her chin, she narrowed her eyes at him. "Part of the reason I came here was because you and I should get to know each other because you're the father of my child. We need to start that process. I'm not going to be here forever."

"You're not," he said, lifting a dark brow. "Is there somewhere you'd rather be?" he asked.

The south of France, a small town in Italy, a Greek island. Somewhere she could rest, somewhere she wouldn't have to answer to her brother, somewhere she could plan her and her baby's future. Somewhere she could disappear for a while. At the moment, Zach's ranch was perfect. That would change as soon as the paparazzi showed up.

"I haven't had time to make plans," she said. "I need to figure out what's best for my child and for me."

"Is it not best for your child to have access to his or her father?" he challenged.

"In most circumstances, that would be best," she conceded. "But the longer I stay here, the more I realize I don't know that much about you."

He lifted his lips in a dangerous grin. "Are you afraid I'm a bad influence?"

Her heart fluttered at the bad boy expression on his face, but she refused to give in to his charm. "As you Americans would say, the jury is out. I need to know more. You haven't been around much." She couldn't resist a wicked urge to goad. "Do I frighten you?"

Flames lit his eyes and he held her gaze as he moved closer to her. "Frighten?" he echoed in a low, deliberate voice.

She felt a twist of fear wrench through her, but she refused to give in to it. She gave the shrug that had been bred into her through generations of royals. "What else should I think?"

Stepping closer, close enough to lower his mouth to hers, he continued to hold her gaze as he gave a husky laugh. "I was giving you some space," he said. "If you're sure you're ready to take me on, I'm here, Princess."

Her stomach dipped at the sensual attraction echoing from him to her and back again. She cleared her throat. "Perhaps after you're finished for the day," she suggested.

"Dinner," he said. "I'll have Hildie fix something for us. We can have dinner in my suite so we won't be interrupted."

Her heart fluttered. "I'm not sure that would be a good

idea," she said, feeling a strong urge to back track, but trying to hold firm.

"Do you need a chaperone?" he challenged.

She stifled her protests. "Of course not," she said. "I'll see you tonight."

Chapter Six

Zach sat across from Tina in what she assumed was the outer room of his bedroom suite. Although the door was closed, she couldn't help feeling curious about what his bedroom looked like. She wondered if she could learn more about him by seeing more of his most personal space.

This room appeared to offer a combination of business and pleasure. They sat at a small dark wood table by one of the large bay windows. The view featured rolling hills of land that stretched as far as the eye could see. It occurred to Tina, that in a way, Zach could survey his kingdom from this window every day.

On the other side of the room sat a large desk with a flat-screen monitor, computer and other electronic equipment. In the center of the room, a plush brown leather sofa sat across from a flat wide-screen TV mounted on the wall.

"Missing the palace?" Zach asked as he stabbed a bite of steak.

"Not really," she said.

He lifted an eyebrow in doubt. "You sure about that? I wondered if this place might seem a little rustic in comparison."

"Well, it's not full of French antiques and the floors aren't marble, but it's far from rustic. You need to remember that I lived in Texas while I went to college. My first two years, I stayed in a dormitory. Not exactly the lap of luxury."

"True enough," he said.

"Plus, I've traveled all over the world and have stayed in places without air conditioning or with limited heat and water." She frowned. "I'm not a total sissy."

He paused, surprise glinting in his eyes, then he gave a low laugh. "Okay," he conceded. "No sissies in this room."

Mollified, she relaxed slightly and picked at her food. "I have enjoyed the quiet," she said. "And the lack of paparazzi has been wonderful, although I'm sure that won't last when they find out where I am."

"They already know," he said. "I've closed the gates and put a couple of men with rifles at the edge of my property."

"Really? I had no idea."

"No need for you to know. You're recovering and—" He shrugged. "Gestating. Those Europeans back off when they've got a rifle pointed in their direction."

"I'm not really that fragile," she protested.

"Hey, you just said it was great to get a break from the paparazzi."

"True," she said and took a bite. The steak was delicious, but her appetite had been iffy lately. She took a sip of water to wash the bite down and studied the hard planes of Zach's face. There was so much she didn't know about him.

"Well, I suppose this is a good time for us to get to know each other better. Although, you could do an internet search on me and find out quite a bit," she added wryly.

"Yeah, age, education, pedigree. Gossip about potential marriage partners."

"Trust me, that was only gossip. Only speculation. At one time, my brother was hoping I would accept a proposal from—" She broke off, remembering she should keep that information private, at least for the time being.

"From who?" he prompted.

"State business," she said. "My brother would consider it confidential."

"And you?" he asked. "What would you consider it?"

"Horrifying," she said. "Impossible."

He chuckled and lifted his beer to his lips. "I can see why it didn't work out."

"Well, enough about me. What about you? Any former loves in your past?"

A shadow crossed over Zach's face, and his expression immediately closed. "I don't discuss that part of my past. You want to know about my sister and brother, my business, my ranch, I'll tell you everything you want to know."

"But—" she said. "You just asked about mine."

"I wanted to know if there is anyone else in the picture with you. I can tell you I'm not seeing anyone. That's all you need to know."

Frustrated, stymied, she stared at him. "How am I to know what kind of father you would be?"

"I can ask the same question. How do I know what kind of mother you would be?" he countered.

"Well, that's different," she said, flustered by how he'd turned the tables on her. "You know I'd already begun to make plans to take care of the baby, to raise the child on my own."

"Without letting the child know about the father," he said, a bit of steel slipping into his voice.

"Yes, but I already explained why. It was a one-night stand. It didn't seem fair to hold you responsible."

"Well, there's where you're wrong. I never back down from my responsibilities."

"I can see how you would feel that way," she conceded. "But what I really want to know is your attitude toward children. What are your thoughts about raising them?"

"Children are to be nurtured and protected. I don't believe in raising a hand against a child. There are other ways to teach them, if that's what you're asking. I will be involved with this child," he said. "You can count on it. And if you really want to know what I think about raising a child, I think the parents should do it together," he said, his gaze meeting hers dead-on. "As husband and wife."

Tina's stomach clenched. "Of course, that doesn't apply to us," she said.

He took a slow swallow from his beer and she couldn't help watching his throat work. The sight was surprisingly sensual. Her thoughts caught her off guard.

"Yet," he said and set down his glass.

Shock raced through her and she couldn't keep her eyes from rounding. "Oh, no. You can't be serious," she said. "You don't really think you and I should—" She shook her head.

"Get married," he finished for her and she marveled at how easily the words slid off his tongue. He didn't appear the least bit troubled by the prospect.

"We don't even know each other," she said, desperation growing inside her. "We don't even know if we like each other."

"We can take some time to find out," he said. "You're early in your pregnancy."

Alarm buttons went off inside her brain and Tina stood. "I'm sorry, but I hope I haven't misled you into believing I have any intention of marrying you. I agree that it's a good idea for us to know each other, but—" She shook her head, her throat closing at the very thought.

He stood and reached for her hand. "Stop panicking. We don't do shotgun weddings around her anymore. Well, not often," he amended with a rough chuckle. "I'm not going to force you to do anything. But don't you think our baby deserves to know that we explored the option of marriage? Years from now, when our child asks why we're not married, and he or she will. You can count on it. Don't you want to know, in your heart of hearts that you have tried to give your child everything they could want? Including an on-site father?"

Her heart still frozen in her chest, she bit her lip.

"Breathe," he said.

She forced herself to do as he said. She shook her head and closed her eyes. "Since I found out I was pregnant, I always pictured myself as a single mother, handling this by myself," she whispered.

"Paint a different picture," he said.

She opened her eyes and looked into his.

"One with me in it," he said. "Because whether we get married or not, you're not doing this alone."

The next morning, Zach rose early and drove his jeep out to a fence that needed to be repaired. He stripped down to his T-shirt and got down to work with the sun blazing down on him.

The menial work usually soothed him, but today he couldn't help thinking about Tina. He wondered if he had scared her away. He wondered if she would still be there when he arrived home today.

Couldn't worry about that, he told himself as he strung new wire to fix the fence. He hadn't been deceptive, he'd been real. She would have to choose her course based on what he'd told her and her own thoughts.

He couldn't blame her hesitance. After all, she was a princess. He would never have bedded her if he'd known. That said, she'd bedded him knowing he was a rancher/businessman. What did that say about her?

He liked that she wasn't prejudiced. Despite his pride, he liked that she was determined to vet him. He wished she wasn't so determined *not* to marry him. *That* struck at his pride. What did she find so offensive about him?

He worked nonstop until lunch and finally glanced at his watch. Pulling a bottle of water from his backpack in the car, he noticed a car coming toward him. He squinted his eyes, trying to recognize the driver.

At first, he thought it was Hildie as he identified her car. The car screeched to a stop in front of him and a brunette exited the vehicle with a basket. He immediately identified Tina.

"What are you doing here?" he asked as she walked toward him.

"Bringing lunch," she said. "Hildie told me you're awful about taking a break."

"Hildie's a tattletale," Zach said with a scowl.

"But she tells the truth," Tina said, looking around. "Is there any shade around here?"

"The car is the best bet," he said. "Did you have the AC on during your drive?"

Tina laughed. "In this heat? Of course."

"Good," he said. "Part of surviving our Texas heat is relying on air-conditioning. Don't try to tough it out."

She glanced at his sweat-stained T-shirt. "Looks like you toughed it out. Hope you want a sandwich."

"I'm in," he said, surprised and pleased that she'd found

her way to him. He walked to the car and got inside. "How did you find me?"

"Hildie gave me directions and I have a GPS," she said. "It's an amazing tool. My sister sent me a box with some of my clothes, laptop and other stuff. I'd recently bought a GPS."

"I'm impressed," he said. "I wouldn't have thought a princess would have driven on dirt roads to deliver a sandwich."

She gave him a withering glance. "You clearly need to revise your ideas of what a princess does and doesn't do."

He accepted the sandwich she gave him and took a bite. "Touché," he said after he swallowed.

She took a sip of her water and studied his face. "What made you fix the fence? That task is pretty low on the totem pole."

He shrugged. "I have a ranch manager and I sometimes do the menial stuff to free him up to stay on top of other tasks. I also often have to go into Dallas for our other companies, so I can't commit to ranch duty all the time."

"You sound like a busy man," she said.

"I'm lucky to have several successful businesses," he said with a shrug of his powerful shoulders that distracted her.

She shook her head. "I don't know how you do everything," she said.

"You do what you need to do to get the job done," he said and remembered what he'd learned about how much of the load Tina had carried for the rest of her family. "Maybe you do know what that's about."

Seeing the light of recognition in her eyes, he felt his gut lift a little. "I'm just about finished here. If you like I can take you for a tour of the ranch when I'm done."

"I'd like a tour of your kingdom," she said with a smile that flashed a dimple at him.

He couldn't help grinning in return. "Kingdom?" he echoed. "That's a pretty term for a few acres of scrub and brush."

She shot him a look of disbelief. "You're doing that thing Americans do so well," she said. "Understate. Play humble."

"No play," he retorted. "I'm humble."

She gave a low, not-quite-ladylike chuckle that got under his skin. "And I'm a runway model."

"You could be. With your body," he said.

Her eyes widened in astonishment. He liked that he'd taken her by surprise.

"You are full of—" She took a breath and her lips twitched. "Flattery."

"Not really," he said. "Meet me back at the house."

"I'd rather watch you finish the job," she said.

He felt a forbidden thrill at the idea that the princess wanted to watch him flex his muscles. He wanted to flex a lot more with her. "Go right ahead," he said and stepped out of the car.

Deciding to give her a show worth watching, he stripped off his shirt and finished the repair job. Fifteen more minutes and he was done. He sucked down the rest of his bottle of water.

Strolling to the driver's side of her car, he tapped on the window. "Did I do an okay job?" he asked.

She pressed the button to lower the window and shot him a look of grudging appreciation. "You should leave your shirt on," she said. "It protects you from the sun."

"Are you saying you don't like my body?"

She gave a huff of impatience. "You're insufferable and not at all humble."

Zach chuckled. "You still want to see the ranch?" he asked.

"Yes. I'll meet you at the house," she said and the window slid upward. Seconds later, she spun away, leaving him in her dust. Her speed made him a little nervous, though he wouldn't tell her that. Winning over a princess wasn't going to be the easiest job he'd undertaken, but he was determined.

Zach grabbed a quick shower after he returned to the house and Tina took the apples and bottles of water Hildie offered. Zach descended the stairs with damp hair and wearing fresh clothes.

Her heart stuttered at the sight of him so strong, carrying his muscular frame with confident ease. He was so different than every other man she'd ever had in her life. He wasn't at all intimidated by her position, but he also seemed to respect her as a person. He was protective, but he hadn't forced her into anything. True, he'd pretty much told her he wanted them to get married, and she'd nearly lost her dinner afterward.

The truth was he still hadn't tried to force her. He'd just stated his case and let the truth sit between them. Terrifying, but in many ways, valid. Too valid.

This was a big decision. Damn. Since she'd met Zach, *everything* had been a big decision. She bit the inside of her lip, a technique she'd developed as a child to cover her nerves.

"Okay, your highness, you ready to see my little plot of land?" he asked, his eyes full of sexy humor.

She smiled. "Your kingdom," she corrected.

He chuckled and she allowed him to lead her out the door to his SUV. He ushered her into the car, started it and turned on the AC. "West first. We call it the devil's land. It's the worst," he said. "Nothing grows here," he said as he turned onto a dirt road.

She looked out the window and couldn't deny what he'd said. "Well, it does look a bit dry. No irrigation possibilities, I suppose?"

"Might as well pour water into Death Valley," he said.

She couldn't quite swallow a chuckle. "I love it that you're not trying to sell me. It's so rare."

"What do you mean?" he asked.

"I mean, everywhere I go people always show me the best stuff first and try to hide the bad. This is hideous."

Zach pulled to a stop and put his car into Park. Propping his jaw against his hand, he stared into the distance. "Yeah, in a way. In a way, if you can get through the barren desert, maybe you can make it through anything."

She searched his hard face and saw a dozen emotions. Loss, grief, resolve, strength. She wondered where it all came from and she suspected it wasn't from the scrubby landscape in front of them.

"Do you come here often?" she asked.

"Probably every few months or so," he said. "This kind of place strips you down to the basics. There's nowhere to hide. That's the bad thing. The good thing is maybe you don't need to hide."

She took a moment to absorb his words. What a concept. No need to hide? She tried to remember when she hadn't felt like she needed to hide. When had she felt like she could be herself? Safe?

She felt a whoosh of tense air exhale from her lungs.

"I heard that," he murmured.

She sucked in a quick breath.

"Relax. That's what this place is for. It's base line."

She took a deep breath. "When did you first come here and feel this way?"

He paused a halfbeat. "I was sixteen. Torn between playing football in high school and helping with the ranch. Tough year."

She knew without him saying which he had chosen. "You gave up football."

He glanced at her. "How'd you know?"

She shrugged. "Just an instinct." She met his gaze. "You and I have more in common that most people might think."

"In what way?" he asked.

"You chose family, duty, heritage. So did I," she said.

"Not entirely," he said. "When you needed to make a change, you did. That's courageous."

She bit the inside of her lip. "Maybe," she said. "Maybe just necessary."

"It's still courageous," he said. "You went against the grain. Against what was expected of you. Don't underestimate yourself, Tina. I don't. No one else should either."

Feeling a rush of pleasure surge through her, she stared into his eyes and felt herself sinking with each breath. Her gaze slipped to his mouth and she felt a tingling sensation on her lips. It felt like a thousand years ago that he'd kissed her, yet she remembered it as if it had happened yesterday.

Confused by her strange combination of feelings, she struggled with the dipping sensation in her stomach. She took a quick breath to clear her head and smiled. "I love it that we started here. What's next?"

"It gets greener," he said, putting the truck in gear and turning around.

He drove past the swimming hole where he learned how to swim, then past a field of bluebonnets, then past his parents', his grandparents', and his great grandparents' graves. She wanted to get out, but he shook off her suggestion to linger. They passed fields and fields of cattle, then he came to another stop, this one overlooked rolling green hills. Looking at the beautiful vista, she felt something inside her ease. "Nice," she murmured.

"Yeah, it does the same thing to me," Zach said.

She studied his face and saw the same peace she felt inside

her. "You're in love with your kingdom," she said, unable to keep a smile from her face.

He did a double take and lifted a dark eyebrow. "In love with my kingdom? That's a first," he said.

"You are," she insisted. "You're as devoted as my brother is, except not as arrogant, thank goodness."

He shook his head. "I wouldn't call myself in love. Maybe committed. Maybe I need to be committed," he muttered under his breath.

"Here's the important question. On your worst day, would you want to be doing anything other than taking care of your ranch?"

He searched her face. "Where did you come up with that?"

"Someone in a very poor village in Africa once told me that on her worst day she wouldn't want to be doing anything else. It was so wise. So magical. I've always wanted to find something that made me feel so strongly."

"So being a princess didn't do it for you?" he asked.

She hesitated, swamped by guilt. "No, it didn't. I don't want to be ungrateful—"

"You're not," he said, covering her hand with his. "You're just being honest. I like that," he said, his gaze wrapping around her heart and squeezing. "I like that a lot."

Chapter Seven

The next morning when Tina awakened, she found a note from Zach under her door. *Eat an early dinner. I'm taking you to town for a meeting at 6:00 p.m.—Zach*

The abrupt language jarred her after the tour of the ranch they'd shared yesterday. He clearly hadn't learned the proper way of addressing royals, she thought wryly recalling all the invitations to her that had read, *The honor of your attendance would be greatly appreciated...* Oh, well, maybe that was part of the reason he appealed to her. Nothing fake or flowery about him. He put his motives flat out in front of her.

After giving her sister Bridget some tips for her upcoming appearances via e-mail, Tina sat in the swing on the front porch, contemplating her and her baby's future with no lightning bolts of decision.

Hildie must have known about the appointment because she called Tina in for early dinner. "Do you know what this meeting is about?"

Hildie glanced at her in surprise. "Meeting?" she echoed. "Zach's taking you into town for an appointment with Dr. McAllister. Dr. McAllister's the best ob-gyn doctor in the area." Hildie shook her head. "We just wish she would have moved to town sooner."

Tina frowned, feeling more than a ripple of indignation. "Are you telling me that Zach plans to choose my doctor? If the royal doctors aren't going to deliver the baby, then I think I should be the one—"

"—It's just a checkup," Zach said from behind her. "Don't most pregnant women visit the doctor by the fourth month?"

"Yes, but the doctor usually just confirms the pregnancy and gives prenatal vitamins. I've been taking prenatal vitamins since I realized I was pregnant. I didn't want the information to be leaked. Unfortunately not everyone at a medical office is discreet."

"That's why I pulled a few strings and arranged an after-hours appointment," Zach said from the doorway. "Are you done?"

Glancing down at her half-eaten meal, she suddenly lost her appetite. "Yes, I am."

"Okay. Let's go."

"Don't you want anything to eat?" she asked.

He shook his head. "I'm not hungry."

Me either, she thought, and picked up her plate as she rose.

"I can get that," Hildie said, taking the plate from her hands. "Are you sure you don't want me to save something for you? Didn't you like it?"

"It was delicious as always, but I'm full, thank you," Tina said.

"Alrighty," Hildie said. "If you change your mind after your appointment, I'll have something waiting for you."

Moments later, Zach helped her into his SUV. She felt a mixture of relief and anticipation. She'd wanted to visit a doctor, but the thought of dealing with leaks had made her hesitant, so she'd researched the most healthy approach toward pregnancy and strictly taken her vitamins.

"What do you know about this doctor?" she asked after they'd driven several miles and the silence stretched between them.

"She's experienced with routine and high-risk pregnancies and deliveries. She's new to the area and we're lucky to get her. We had to recruit her," he said.

"Who is we?" she asked.

"The community," he said.

She frowned in confusion. "But who is the community?" she asked. "How does that work? Do all of you get together and put together a special fund?"

"Something like that," he said. "Some of us get together and pool funds for the good of the community."

"Hmm," she said and nodded. "The haves help the have-nots."

"The haves help the haves *and* the have-nots," he corrected. "The whole community."

She studied him for a long moment. "Bet you were on the steering committee for this," she said. "I wonder why."

"Don't," he said and clenched his jaw.

They were silent for the rest of the drive, leaving her to wonder what was going on inside Zachary. He pulled in front of a medical office, and her thoughts turned to her baby. She automatically pressed her hand against her abdomen.

"You ready?" he asked as he cut the engine.

She nodded. "Yes, I am."

He helped her out of the car and they entered the office. Zach knocked on the receptionist's window.

Silence followed.

"Are you sure someone is here?" she asked.

He nodded, but rapped again.

Seconds later, a door whipped open and a tall woman dressed in a white coat with short hair appeared in the doorway. "Looking for me, Mr. Logan? I don't usually take appointments this late, but you made me curious." The woman glanced in Tina's direction. "I'm Dr. McAllister."

"I'm Valentina…"

Dr. McAllister wrinkled her brow. "A lot of names and they're not southern. I'll take a wild guess. Royal and pregnant?"

A rush of self-consciousness rose from her feet up to her cheeks. "Yes. As a matter of fact, I am," she murmured.

"No need for embarrassment. Pregnancy in all its forms, planned or a big surprise, is my business. I'm here to make everything go as smooth as silk. You're safe with me," Dr. McAllister said.

Tina felt her shoulders relax and a soothing sensation seep through her. "I would appreciate it."

Dr. McAllister shrugged. "I wouldn't have it any other way. Come back for the examination." She glanced at Zach. "I'll call you to come back if necessary. Otherwise, feel free to pace the waiting room."

With a quietly reassuring nurse by her side, Dr. McAllister conducted the examination. The nurse took a vial of blood to double-check Tina's iron. The doctor set her stethoscope over Tina's abdomen and Tina heard the baby's heartbeat. The sound filled her with wonder.

"I'll do this for Zachary even though he's a pain in the butt," the doctor said. "Marie, could you please bring in Mr. Logan?"

"This will be cold," Dr. McAllister said and squirted goop on Tina's abdomen.

Tina twitched at the sensation. The doctor pressed a device over her abdomen.

"Look at the screen," the doctor said.

Tina stared at the monitor and saw a miniature combination of tiny arms and limbs with a large head and a beating heart. "It looks like an alien."

"Is it healthy?" Zach asked, walking into the room.

Hearing his voice, Tina swung her head to look at him. He looked so tense. His jaw and his fists were clenched.

"Looks very healthy so far," Dr. McAllister said. "Sex? I can't guarantee, but if I were a betting woman, I would say this is a girl. We'll know more with the next ultrasound."

A thrill raced through Tina. Even though she'd known she was pregnant and had been as healthy as possible, the fact that she was carrying a baby hadn't felt real until now. The realization took her breath away. "Wow. A baby," she whispered. "She's a real little person."

"A healthy baby," Zach said.

She met his gaze and he took her hand. Watching him stare at their baby on the screen, Tina had the bone-deep feeling that nothing between them would ever be the same.

After repeated assurances from Dr. McAllister that both Tina and the baby were healthy, Tina and Zach left the office. He helped her into the truck and they both sat silently for a long moment.

"That ultrasound was amazing," she said. "Amazing."

He nodded and his lips lifted a notch. "Yeah, it was." He studied her for a moment. "Would you like to get some ice cream?"

"That sounds wonderful," she said and remembered when they'd gotten a float after the masquerade party. She glanced around the empty parking lot then looked back at him. "I'm impressed. No paparazzi in sight."

"Like I said, I pulled some strings," he said and started

the car. "Dr. McAllister will be discreet, but you won't be able to hide the pregnancy soon."

"I know," she said, feeling the weight of her position settle on her again. "I'm just hoping to buy a little more time so I can figure out my plans and how to announce them."

"Heard any more from your brother or sisters?" he asked.

"Angry text and voice mail messages. I haven't picked up because I don't want their upset cluttering my mind. I feel as if my staying at your ranch is a rare opportunity I need to pursue to the fullest. I can't do that if I'm feeling guilty about how my family is handling my absence."

"Good choice," he said. "You need to put your well-being and the baby's health first. If they can't understand that, it's their problem. And if you'd like me to answer for you—"

"No, no," she said, unable to fight a combination of pleasure and humor at his defense of her. "Have you always been this protective about women who were important to you?"

"You're carrying my child," he said. "How else could I be?"

She felt a sharp twinge of disappointment. "Oh," she said. "So, if I weren't pregnant, you would be more detached."

He tossed a sideways glance at her full of heat and passion. "I've never acted detached toward you, Princess. Not from the first time we met."

Her heart leapt at the sensual growl in his voice. She still couldn't figure him out. She still had so many questions and she wasn't sure how to get her answers. Tina knew, however, that she wanted to know much more about Zach.

"Favorite ice cream?" she asked impulsively.

"Vanilla," he said.

"Oh, that's so—"

"Boring," he said for her and his lips lifted in a secret grin. "Bet yours is chocolate."

"Times three," she said. "Favorite color?"

"Blue, like cornflowers or the ocean," he said.

"But you're landlocked," she pointed out.

"Doesn't mean I don't like to visit," he said. "What about you?"

"Blue, too. It makes me feel peaceful. Favorite dessert?"

"Apple pie," he said. "Yours is chocolate something."

"Mousse," she said. "Chocolate mousse. But there've been times when I was visiting a third world country on the behalf of Chantaine and I was extremely grateful for Nutella."

He chuckled. "I bet you were."

"What do you think about girls playing football?" she asked.

"Not mine," he said.

"What if she could run like a jaguar, kick a ball into next month?"

"Not my daughter," he said implacably.

"Because football's not ladylike?" she asked.

"Because I don't want her hurt," he said. "She can pick a noncontact sport. If I had a son, I would warn him off professional sports too. Injuries can cut your career plans in a second."

"Hmm. That's still a bit sexist," she said.

He pulled into the parking lot of the ice cream parlor. "Are you telling me you would be okay with your little girl growing up and playing pro football?"

"No," she said.

He nodded. "No need for argument."

"But I wouldn't want my little boy playing football either," she said. "It's a primitive sport."

He grinned and slid his finger over her mouth. "Good thing we're starting out with a girl."

After the doctor's appointment, Tina felt closer to Zach. She felt a tie with him that she hadn't felt before. It made her think of him when she awakened in the morning, in the afternoon and at night before she went to sleep.

She'd felt such a connection to him. When she'd confessed her dissatisfaction with her duties as a royal representative, his lack of condemnation had made something inside her ease. She'd felt almost hopeful that perhaps she could find something that filled her heart in the future.

But Zach was nowhere in sight. He was like a ghost. After two days, she wondered if she'd imagined her time with him.

After the third day, she awakened, stepped from her bed to look out the window, wishing she could see him, but somehow knowing she wouldn't. Tina looked out onto the rolling hills and felt a mixture of emotions. Longing, desperation, hope...

Not wanting to dwell on any of these feelings, she hit the shower and got dressed. She was determined to beat Hildie before she brought breakfast. Pounding down the steps, she found Hildie on the phone.

"You don't say," Hildie said and silence followed.

"That's terrible," Hildie continued and shook her head. "We'll do something, Hannah. We sure won't leave the Gordons hungry."

A moment later, Hildie hung up the phone and sighed. "Those Gordons. It couldn't happen at a worse time."

"What's wrong?" Tina asked.

"The Gordons, our neighbors," Hildie said. "Their house burned down. One of the barns burned down too."

"That's horrible," she said. "Do they have children? How large is their family?"

"Six including Sheree's mother. Sheree's the wife. Bob Gordon, her husband, is a rancher. They have three kids." Hildie shook her head. "And another on the way. I think Sheree is due any moment."

"No family in the area?" Tina asked.

"None with enough room to take them in."

"Then they should come here," Tina insisted.

Hildie gawked at her. "Oh, Miss—" She broke off. "Your highlyness—"

"Please don't call me that," Tina said, cringing. "This makes perfect sense. The Gordons need a place to sleep. There's plenty of room here," she said, extending out her arms.

Hildie looked hesitant. "Zachary Logan is generous, but he has always wanted his privacy. He insists on it," she said.

"I can't believe he would withhold shelter from someone in such need," Tina said.

Hildie shook her head again. "I can't make that call. You'll have to talk to Zach."

Tina was surprised by Hildie's reluctance. Hildie was usually vocal with her opinions and how she thought everything should be.

"I'll do that," Tina said, "but we should get guest rooms ready."

Hildie blinked. "Alrighty," she said. "But I'm telling you that you better talk to Zach or there's going to be big trouble."

"As you wish. But if I can't reach him by cell, I'll need to use the car," Tina said, because she'd learned that cell service wasn't always reliable at the far reaches of the ranch.

Hildie winced. "I'm not sure that's a good idea."

"I need the car, please," she insisted, using her best royal voice.

Hildie frowned. "Alrighty," she said. "But I'm going on record as claiming no responsibility."

Tina gave a quick nod. "Thank you very much. I'll take the keys."

After failed attempts at reaching Zach by cell, Tina asked

where Zach was and drove in the direction of the south pasture, but she couldn't find him. She drove down several dirt roads and finally came upon several men outside a barn. She pulled alongside the barn and got out of the car.

"Hello. How are you? Is Zach here?" she asked.

The men looked at her as if she were an alien. "Zach?"

"Yes," she said. "Zachary Logan. I need to speak with him."

One of the men rested his hand on a rake and stared at her. "Who are you?"

She felt a frisson of uneasiness, but didn't give in to it. "I'm Valentina Devereaux."

The one who'd asked her name stepped forward and dipped his head. "I'm Ray and I'm sorry, but Zach left here about an hour ago. I think he was going to the next field, east," he said. "But I can't be sure."

Tina sighed. "Thank you very much, sir. If you should see him, please tell him to contact me."

"We'll do that, ma'am," Ray said and tipped his hat.

Tina climbed into the car and headed east. She came upon another barn where one man stood outside. Stopping her car, she stepped out of her car. "Hello. How are you?" she asked. "I'm looking for Zachary Logan. Have you seen him?"

The man shook his head. "I'm looking for him too. He's supposed to stop by here sometime today. You want to leave a message?"

Impatient with trying to track Zachary down, Tina returned to the car to grab a piece of paper and a pen. "Yes, I do. I'm Tina," she said. "And you are?"

"Fred," he said.

"Lovely to meet you, Fred," she said and scribbled a note to Zachary. "Could you please give this to Zachary? Please tell him to call me if he has any questions," she said, handing him the piece of paper.

"I can do that," Fred said, dipping his head. "If you need anything you can give me a call," he said and gave her a business card. "Cell phone number is on the bottom, although as you probably know, the service around here is a little sketchy."

"Exactly," she said, pocketing Fred's card. "Thank you very much."

"My pleasure," Fred said and Tina got into the car with an invigorated sense of purpose. Surely Hildie was mistaken that Zach would have a problem giving the Gordons a place to stay. Zach would want to help his neighbors.

Tired and achy from a long day outside filling in for one of his managers, all Zach wanted was a hot shower, a hot meal and a quiet evening. He stepped inside the mudroom to ditch his boots. His mind flitted to Tina as it often did lately. He wasn't quite sure how to handle the woman. How to keep her at the ranch without her getting under his skin.

A loud shriek caught him off guard. "What the—" He strode down the hallway to sounds coming from the den. Turning a corner, he quickly took in the sight of his very pregnant neighbor, Sheree Gordon, sitting on the couch, an elementary-school age boy sitting in *Zach's* chair working the remote to his large flat-screen TV and Tina sitting on the floor with two small children.

Hildie walked into the den. "Supper's ready. Everyone wash up and—" She caught sight of Zach and immediately stopped.

Tina glanced up at Hildie, then looked at Zach. Rising to her feet with the two little children still clinging to her hands, she met his gaze. "Well, there you are, stranger. I tried to call you several times on your cell today."

Zach pulled his phone from his pocket and noticed his

message sign was on. "I was out of range for most of the day."

"That's what I heard, so I drove out to find you. No luck, so I left a message with a man named Fred," she said.

"Yeah, I didn't get to him today," he said.

"Oops," Tina said.

Sheree stood and eased the children away from Tina. "Yes, I know you're having fun with your new friend, but it's time to wash your hands for dinner." She looked at Zach. "I can't tell you how much we appreciate your letting us stay here with you for a few days. You and Tina are too generous for words."

Stay here? he thought and blinked. *Here in my house?*

"I mean, I'm due in a couple of weeks and my mother is recovering from knee surgery. The fire totally wiped us out." Sheree's eyes filled with tears. "Bob and I will never be able to repay you for helping us."

Zach had heard about the fire at the Gordon ranch and he'd planned to help in some way—maybe help put the family up in a hotel for a few nights, provide a few meals and some clothes. But not this.

The youngest child, a toddler who was a girl, gave a high-pitched shriek that lit his nerve endings like a stream of firecrackers on the Fourth of July.

Sheree winced. "Sorry, she's at the screaming stage, and being in a different place make it worse. Come on, Amy and Doug. Matthew, turn off the TV. Time to get ready for dinner."

"Mooooom," the older boy complained.

"Now," Sheree said firmly and Matt rose from the chair.

After his new guests left the room, Zach met Tina's gaze. "In the future, if you're going to invite people to stay here, I'd appreciate it if you would let me know."

"I tried, but you weren't accessible," Tina said.

"You could have waited until I got home just now," he said.

"No, I couldn't. This family has been through a devastating experience. Someone had to act quickly."

"Where did you put all of them?" he asked.

"Oh, that was easy. I put Sheree and Bob in the guest room at the front of the house, Matt in the upstairs den on the foldout sofa. We're putting Sheree's mom in the downstairs library so she won't have to take the stairs. And the two little ones will go in the room next to mine. It's such a lovely little room with the seat at the bay window and built-in shelves. I was surprised to find it completely empty," she said, confusion wrinkling her brow. "I asked Hildie about it, but the phone rang and we got busy."

Zach's gut twisted into a knot. That room had been for his baby. His baby who had died. A flash of anger rushed through him. What right did Tina have to invade that room? He'd donated the furniture to a charitable organization, but every time he went into that room, he felt the loss well up inside him again, fresh and painful.

Clenching his jaw, he swallowed over a knot in the back of his throat. "Don't do this again," he told her. "Not without talking with me first."

She searched his face. "You're angry. Why?" she asked. "This is only for a short time. Is your privacy so important that you can't—"

He lifted his hand. "Enough. I don't want to discuss it anymore."

"But how can I understand—"

"You understand to talk to me first. That's all you need to understand."

Clearly not satisfied, Tina frowned then sighed. "Well, I suppose I should also tell you that we're holding a community barbecue here tomorrow night so that neighbors can come and donate replacement clothing, furniture and household goods for the Gordons."

Zach dipped his head in disbelief. "Tomorrow night?"

She nodded. "Through my diplomatic experiences in disaster areas, I've learned that one really must move on this kind of thing right away. People forget and needs are left unmet."

Hearing her use the word diplomatic made something inside him click. "This is a princess thing, isn't it?"

She shot him a wary look. "Princess thing?"

He nodded. "Now I get it. This is the kind of thing you used to do in your country, except maybe on a grander scale. If this is going to be your M.O., then you and I are definitely going to need to have a talk. It will have to wait until later, though, since we have *guests*."

Tina stared at Zachary Logan's broad back as he walked away. She felt a deep sinking sensation inside her as she realized she had imposed upon Zach and clearly offended him.

He appeared weary and frustrated, and now she'd caused a situation where he couldn't be at ease even in his own home. Guilt suffused her. Hildie had warned her, but Tina had brushed the woman's concerns aside.

She had followed her natural instincts when she'd heard about the Gordons' tragedy. Plus, taking care of the Gordons had allowed her to take her attention off of her confusing feelings for Zach.

Hearing the approaching stampede of the Gordon children, Tina had no time to dwell on her regret. She helped Hildie serve the meal and feed the children. Afterward, Sheree offered to help clean up, but Hildie and Tina insisted the woman go rest.

"The poor woman has been through enough during the

last twenty-four hours," Tina murmured as she helped remove the dishes from the table.

"So true," Hildie said, then only the sound of clattering dishes filled the kitchen.

"You were right," Tina said in a low voice, full of misery. "Zach is angry. He was very upset that I invited the Gordons without discussing it with him first. I should have considered his feelings. I just assumed he would want to help—"

"Now, don't you be getting the wrong idea. There's no man more generous than Zachary Logan. He's always one to help out when someone needs it. He helped fund my niece's college education. The man is extremely generous," Hildie said then sighed. "But everyone has their soft spots. This home is Zachary's cave. Having this place has gotten him through some rough times."

"What rough times?" Tina asked. "I know the deaths of his parents must have been difficult, but I sense there's something more. But he won't discuss it with me. Tell me, please."

Hildie shook her head. "It's not my place."

So frustrated she could scream, Tina tamped down her feelings and finished helping Hildie in silence. All the while, her mind was going a mile a minute. This was ridiculous. How were she and Zach ever going to be able to communicate effectively if she didn't know what had caused him so much pain? She had to find out. She formulated a plan. The day after tomorrow, she was going into Dallas and she was going to get some answers.

"I'm going to heat up a plate for Zach and take it upstairs," Hildie said.

"I'll do it," Tina offered.

Hildie shot her a skeptical glance. "Are you sure that's a good idea? He's probably as cranky as a bear with a sore paw."

"Since I caused the injury, I should make amends," Tina

said, stiffening her back. She knew full well that Zach would likely give her the cold shoulder.

After heating the full plate of food, she grabbed two ice cold beers from the refrigerator and climbed the stairs to his suite. Gently tapping on his door, she stood and waited. No answer. She tapped again, this time more loudly.

The door swung slightly open and Zachary stood there wearing a towel slung around his hips and, she supposed, nothing else. His hair looked ebony from the wetness. His eyelashes surrounded his blue eyes in spikes of black and water droplets dotted his wide shoulders and muscular pecs. Her gaze drifted downward to the fine hair that arrowed down his flat abdomen.

All male, all man, she thought, her stomach dipping to her feet as she remembered that night they'd shared together. It had been months ago, she reminded herself. And everything was different now.

"Is that for me?" he asked, pointing to the plate she held.

She nodded. "Yes, yes, it is."

"Bring it in and I'll put on some clothes," he said and she followed him inside his suite. Domain, she corrected herself. Definitely his domain, she thought as she couldn't resist the urge to shoot a searching glance past the open door into his bedroom. Huge bed, she noticed. Sheepskin rugs surrounding the edge of the bed. Bedside table with a lamp and a couple of books. She wondered what he was reading. Was it for pleasure or business? Since she'd come to the ranch, Zach had seemed all business. She'd seen another side of him. Had that been a complete anomaly?

Wearing a half-unbuttoned shirt and a pair of jeans, he reentered his office/living room. "Thanks for the food. I'm assuming both beers are for me since you're not drinking?"

he said more than asked with a wry suggestion of a grin. "You thought I might need more than one?"

He popped the top on the first bottle and waved toward the sofa for her to sit. Taking a seat opposite her, he placed the plate on the table beside him.

Surprised at his lack of hostility, she lifted her shoulders in confusion. "You seemed tired and I don't think I helped matters. I apologize for taking matters into my own hands."

"I imagine it's what you've always done," he said and dug into his meal.

She opened her mouth to protest then changed her mind. "Within certain parameters," she said. "There were always the opinions of advisers and my brother."

"Bet that drove you crazy. Always having to answer to someone. Would have driven me crazy," he said and took a long swallow from his beer. "My middle name isn't Grinch or Scrooge just because I like a little notice when my house is gonna be turned into a temporary hotel."

Tina felt another twist of regret. "I know that. Again, I apologize. It's not as if this is my home. It's yours."

He met her gaze for a long moment that made her heart skip over itself. "We'll see," he said. "I talked with Bob, Sheree's husband, then I talked with Doyle, a friend of mine in Dallas. Doyle's into everything and he happens to have a large mobile home the Gordons can use until their house is rebuilt. Should be ready in two days."

Tina dropped her jaw in surprise. "Two days? My goodness, that's fast. How in the world did you—"

He rubbed his jaw. "You give me a couple minutes to think and a shower, and I'm good."

"Thank you. I'm sure the whole family will be thrilled."

"I don't know about Matthew. He looked like he was getting attached to my chair and my remote."

She laughed in agreement then silence descended between

them. "Is there anything else I can get for you?" she asked, rising.

He rose to his feet too and shook his head. "No, I'm hitting the sack. You should do the same. Tomorrow's gonna be a long one."

She walked to the door and turned around, startled to find him mere inches from her.

He lifted his hand to her chin. "I mean what I say. Part of the reason you came here was to rest."

She nodded, determined to ignore the way her heart was pounding in her chest. "Yes, I've done that."

He paused a half-beat. "So you don't need any more rest now?"

She glanced. "Too much rest is boring," she said. "Tell me you don't agree. That is," she added meaningfully, "if you've ever actually rested more than a few hours."

"Yeah, I get you. I had appendicitis and that recovery drove me crazy. But I'm not pregnant and you are," he said, stroking her jaw again. "Don't overdo it."

"I thought I wasn't going to have to take orders since I'm away from my country," she said with a sigh.

"I won't be giving you the same kind of orders your brother does," he said. "You can count on that."

Chapter Eight

"And why wasn't I invited?" Daniel Logan asked as Zach flipped burgers on the large gas grill.

Zach glanced up from the grill, surprised to see his brother. "Hey, what are you doing here?" he asked, since Daniel lived in Dallas.

"I was out this way because I'm looking into buying some land—"

Zach stared in amazement at his younger brother. "You? Land? You swore you'd never do any kind of ranching again."

"Yeah, well, we'll see," Daniel said evasively, glancing around at the crowd. "What's going on here?"

"It's a cookout," Zach said in a dry tone. "Can't you tell? Or have you forgotten since you only eat inside restaurants these days?"

Daniel shot him a sideways glance. "What's the deal? You barely ever invite me out here. Now you're throwing a big neighborhood party."

"It's not really a party. It's a charity thing, and I didn't throw it," Zach said, glancing across the large backyard at Tina fluttering from one person to the next, charming each of them. "It got thrown on me."

"What do you—" Daniel broke off as he gazed in the same direction as Zach. "A woman," he said in amazement. "You mentioned something a few weeks ago on the phone about a complication, but you didn't say it was a woman. When did you meet her? Does she live in town or out here? I can't remember seeing her before."

"If you can shut off your diarrhea of the mouth for just a moment, I'll explain," Zach said, although explaining Tina wasn't the easiest thing in the world. "Tina and I met a few months ago and got along—" He cleared his throat. "Pretty well."

Daniel gave a low laugh. "How well?"

"Well enough that she's pregnant," Zach said.

Daniel did a double take first at Zach, then at Tina. "Damn. I couldn't tell at first from how the dress fit her, but, yeah." He turned back to Zach. "What are you gonna do?"

Zach sighed, moving the cooked burgers onto the buns. "She's staying at the ranch. That's a first step."

"First?" Daniel said. "Sounds like you two skipped a few along the way. You gonna marry her?"

"I'm working on it," he said. "She's not from Texas."

"Where's she from?" Daniel asked.

"Chantaine."

"Where the hell is that?"

"It's a small principality in the Mediterranean," he said and decided to drop the rest of the bomb. "Tina's a princess."

Daniel gawked at him then swore. "A princess?" His brother shook his head and looked in Tina's direction, giving a hearty laugh. "Thank God."

Zach frowned. "What do you mean thank God?"

Daniel's face turned serious. "I mean you've been stuck in a rut since Jenny and the baby..." He lifted his hand when Zach opened his mouth. "You asked, so let me finish. You had every right to mourn. Every right. But you've become a crabby hermit. I have a feeling this woman is going to turn your world upside down."

Zach took a long look at Tina and felt his gut twist and turn. She laughed and the sound felt like honey sliding through him. When he'd arrived home last night to a full house of overnight visitors, he'd been damn sure that he and Tina would never be compatible. His privacy and solitude were too important to him.

Her energy and determination, her heart, however, did something to him. She inspired him to want to help too. To maybe do something he didn't usually do, such as flip burgers for the multitudes so they could donate what they could to help the Gordons.

On top of that, his physical attraction to her hadn't waned one bit. In fact, it had gotten worse. Tonight, he'd seen other men smiling and flirting with her and he suddenly found himself making a fist or clenching his jaw. One of his men had asked if he could take her out to dinner because he hadn't known she belonged to Zach.

The truth was she didn't belong to Zach and that bothered the hell out of him.

Hours later, after a couple of Zach's workers hustled out the last guests, Zach watched Tina sink onto a bench and walked toward her. Handing her a cold bottle of water, he noticed the signs of weariness and felt a twist of concern. "You pushed a little too hard and too long tonight, didn't you?"

She accepted the bottle of water and took a long swallow. "Not really. I think it was just that last hour when the news that I was a princess seemed to run through the crowd like wildfire." She shook her head. "I really didn't want the focus taken off of the Gordons' plight."

Zach couldn't resist a low chuckle. "You can't really blame them. We don't get a lot of royalty around here. That's why I made the announcement that the party was over and sent a few of my men to help people move along."

She shot him a sheepish look. "I guess I couldn't stay incognito forever."

He sat down beside her. "No. The paparazzi have been trying to get past my gate since you first got here. Folks around here are usually busy enough that they don't pay a lot of attention to the gossip rags, but finding out you were here tonight, everyone was curious. The good news is they'll eventually calm down."

"How do you know they will?" she asked.

"After the initial fascination wears off, they'll be a lot more interested in what kind of person you are instead of whether you have a title or not."

"If I stay," she said in a soft voice.

His gut twisted at her words. "Yeah. How do you like it so far?"

He saw several different emotions cross her face. "I'm still finding my way. As much as I needed the rest when I arrived, I know I'll have to do something. I would go out of my mind with boredom if I did nothing all day long."

Although Zach would prefer that Tina do nothing all day long so he could be assured that she and the baby were safe, he understood her dilemma. "I can understand that. I would feel the same way. Maybe you could take a little time to figure out exactly what you would like to do. You have choices here."

She gave a long exhale. "Choices. You have no idea what the possibility of making my own choices does to me."

"You're right," he said. "I don't because I've been making my choices for a long time. I think it's high time you get to follow your heart. You've got a good one," he said.

She met his gaze and her skin looked so soft in the moonlight that he couldn't resist touching her cheek. "You think so?" she said.

"Yeah, I do," he said and gave in to an instinct that had been building inside him since he'd first set eyes on her again. He lowered his head and covered her lips with his mouth.

Hearing her soft intake of breath, he paused but didn't move away. "It's still there, isn't it?" he asked against her lips.

"What?" she whispered, her lips still parted.

"Whatever was between us that night at the masquerade party," he said. "Whatever made me want you and made you want me."

He deepened the kiss, sliding his tongue inside her lips. She welcomed him, drawing him deeper, moving closer to him. Her breasts brushed his chest.

He felt like she'd hit a trip wire. An explosion of need ripped through him. He slid one of his hands down to the back of her waist, urging her body against his. A growl of desire rumbled from his throat.

She must have felt the same fire because she slid her fingers up behind his neck and matched him stroke for stroke in the passionate kiss.

"You should be in my bed," he said, his entire body twisting with need for her.

He felt more than heard her soft intake of breath. "I'm not sure that's a good idea."

He brushed his fingers lightly over one of her breasts where her nipple stood in turgid arousal. "Your body seems to think it's a very good idea."

She pulled back and stared into his eyes, seeming to try

to search his soul. "I'm not a teenager. Despite the fact that I appeared to jump into bed with you without a second thought, that's not my nature."

"I wasn't suggesting that it was," he said. "But you can't deny there's something between us. And it's more than this baby."

She tore her gaze from his and took a deep breath. "Perhaps," she said then opened her eyes. "But not tonight."

Two days later, the Gordons moved into their temporary home and Tina put together a plan for getting her questions answered. As always, first thing in the morning, she flipped through her text messages, shaking her head. "What a nasty temper," she muttered of her brother. "He needs a wife." Then she thought better of it. What woman in her right mind would put up with her brother? "A pet," she thought. "He needs a pet." She texted him the suggestion, then called her friend Keely McCorkle in Dallas. "I'm in town," she said. "May I take you and Caitlyn for lunch or pop in for a visit?"

Keely squealed. "Of course. When did you get here? Why didn't you tell me you were coming? Why aren't you staying with me?"

Tina laughed, feeling a surge of relief at the sound of her friend's voice. She also, however, knew Keely would have even more questions once she saw Tina. "We can talk about that at lunch. Where would you like to meet?"

"Oh, come to my place. I don't want to share you. If we go out in public, they'll be all over you," Keely said.

Thank goodness. "Are you sure I can't bring something?"

"Yes," Keely said. "Yourself. Now hurry up and get here."

Tina smiled. Now all she had to do was talk Hildie into letting her borrow her car.

After her shower, she ate every bite on the plate Hildie gave her even though she feared she would pop. "Hildie, I have a favor to ask you."

Hildie glanced over her shoulder and beamed at Tina's empty plate. "Good job. Now you're starting to eat like a mother-to-be should. How can I help you?"

"If I may, I need to borrow something from you please," Tina said.

Hildie gazed at her expectantly. "What?"

"I have a longtime friend in Dallas. Her name is Keely McCorkle."

"The name's familiar," Hildie said, squinting her eyes thoughtfully. "Brent," she said. "Brent McCorkle. Great guy. Brent and Zach have been friends for a long time."

Tina nodded with a smile. "Yes. I'd like to go into town to visit Keely."

"Shouldn't be a problem. Just give Zachary a call and—"

Tina shook her head. "I want to go today. I want to drive myself."

Hildie stared at her in disbelief. "Oh, hell, no."

Tina met Hildie's gaze without flinching. "I suppose I could rent a car," she said.

Hildie's left eye twitched.

"Or I could…what do you Americans call it? Thumb?"

"Omigod, you wouldn't," Hildie said.

Tina leaned toward Hildie and used her best confidential royal tone. "I *really* want to visit Keely today. And I *really* don't want to be supervised by Zachary."

"Mm, mm, mm," Hildie said with a frown as she sighed. "I'll drive you," Hildie said. "But we have to be back before Zachary returns or he *will* fire me."

An hour later as Hildie drove into the circular drive in front of the McCorkles' home, Tina turned to the woman who had muttered in disapproval for the entire drive. "Are you sure you won't join us?" Tina asked. "I'm certain Keely would love to meet you."

Hildie shook her head. "No. You two go ahead. The sooner you finish your visit, the sooner we can get back to the ranch. Just remember, we must leave by three o'clock."

"Three o'clock," Tina said. "Thank you so very much, Hildie. You have no idea how much this means to me."

Hildie nodded, but muttered under her breath.

Tina closed the passenger door of the car and walked to the front porch. She barely lifted her hand to knock before the door flung open and Keely greeted her with a squeal.

"What a treat!" Keely said, immediately wrapping her arms around Tina. "I still can't believe you were even *thinking* of coming to Texas without telling me first so we could plan a visit. Come on in," she said, taking Tina's hand. "The baby's sleeping, so we have time to gab. Are you hungry? I ordered takeout from that café you enjoyed so much the last time you were here. So tell me what you're doing here," Keely demanded as she pushed Tina into a chair in the kitchen nook lit by skylights. The table was filled with croissant sandwiches, salads and pastries.

"This looks beautiful. You did too much. As for my visit, it's complicated. I'll tell you the story, but I want to hear how you and Brent and Caitlyn are doing first," Tina said, still not exactly sure how to break the news to her best friend in the world. She was relieved Keely hadn't noticed her pregnancy. Tina had deliberately chosen a flowy silk top over white slacks to hide her bump.

Keely beamed. "Caitlyn is perfect. She's sitting up, trying to scoot and crawl. Once she's mobile, I won't get anything done but watch her."

"And Brent?" Tina asked.

"He works too hard, but I hope I can talk him into taking

a break in the fall." She poured iced tea into two tall glasses. "Now tell me about you. I read about Ericka's wedding. It looked like everything turned out beautifully. I know that was due to you. Is she doing okay?"

"She's doing great. She seems very happy. I visited her right before I came to the States," she said.

Keely frowned. "It's usually all over the news when you arrive, but I don't recall seeing anything. Although I confess I just got back from visiting my mother in Aspen."

"That's great. Did you take Caitlyn with you?"

"Of course," Keely said. "I would have never heard the end of it if I hadn't."

It occurred to Tina, for the first time, that her child wouldn't have the gift of grandparents. The twist of sadness caught her by surprise.

Keely covered her hand, her brow wrinkled in concern. "Hey, are you okay? You seem a little on edge."

Tina took a deep breath. No time like the present. "The last time I was here, I met your friend Zachary Logan."

Keely nodded. "That's right. We asked him to look after you and then you didn't show up until the next morning. Brent and I were both going to clobber him for not keeping track of you, but we haven't seen him since the masquerade party."

"Well," Tina said, clearing her throat. "He actually did keep track of me. We spent the night together."

Keely's eyes rounded. "Oh." She turned silent, a rarity for Keely. "You and Zachary," she said, shaking her head. "You're so responsible and he's so…well, still in mourning after all these years."

Tina's stomach knotted. "Mourning? Over his parents?"

"I'm sure he was sad when they passed, but no—" Keely shook her head and broke off. "He just can't seem to get over his wife and baby. I can't totally blame him…."

Tina heard nothing after *wife and baby*. "Wife?" she echoed.

Keely met her gaze and nodded. "I guess you don't know. There's no reason you should unless you'd gotten to know Zachary better. He lost his wife, Jenny, and their unborn child due to complications from her pregnancy. He totally shut himself off after it happened. We had to call in favors to get him to attend the masquerade. He always has an excuse. Brent told me he wouldn't even confide in his brother and sister."

Shell-shocked, Tina tried to absorb the information. So this was what neither Zachary nor Hildie would discuss. This was why Zachary had been so upset when she'd invited the Gordon family to stay at his home. This was why he was so determined to do the right thing for the baby. Tina realized that in some ways, by getting pregnant, she was Zach's worst nightmare.

"Tina," Keely said, patting her hand. "You've turned white as a sheet. Tell me what's going on."

Tina met Keely's gaze. "I'm pregnant with Zachary's baby."

Chapter Nine

As the afternoon thunderstorm turned into a torrential downpour, Zachary stomped into the mudroom. He could tell this wasn't going to be a short rain, so he decided to take an early break and return to work later in the afternoon.

Stepping out of his boots, he walked into the hallway listening for sounds of Hildie or Tina. He heard nothing but the tick tock of the old grandfather clock in the front room.

He strode into the kitchen and poured himself a glass of water. Glancing around for a note, again he found none. He did, however, spot Hildie's cell phone on the kitchen counter.

Uneasiness prickled along the back of his neck. "Hildie," he called. "Tina." He climbed the stairs and lightly knocked on the guest room door. Silence followed and he pushed the door open, searching for her. He caught the faintest whiff of her French perfume, but nothing more.

Where were they? he wondered. Hildie wouldn't take Tina

out without letting him know. Hildie knew Zach was trying to keep a clamp on the paparazzi. He rushed downstairs and glanced outside. Hildie's car was gone.

His heart began to pound in his chest. Had there been an emergency? If so, why hadn't they called him? He knew the cell coverage on the ranch was sketchy, but Hildie would have at least left a message. He checked his cell phone and saw messages, but none from his housekeeper. None from Tina.

He wondered if Tina had decided to leave. Had he pushed too hard last night? She'd responded to him. She'd wanted him, but she was holding back. For the sake of their child, she had to stay here with him. The possibility of Tina and their child on the other side of the world made him sweat. How could he keep them safe if they weren't here with him?

Not that he'd been able to keep Jenny and the baby safe, his conscience stabbed at him. Even though the doctor had told him that it wasn't his fault, Zach had never forgiven himself. He punched the speed dial number for Tina's cell phone and counted the rings until he received the automated voice mail response.

He swore. *Where was she?*

"I'm fired," Hildie said, her white knuckled fingers wrapped around the steering wheel as she and Tina sat stuck in a sea of never-ending traffic. Rain pelted down as the windshield wipers furiously moved from one side to the other.

"That's ridiculous," Tina said. "You won't get fired. All you did was drive a guest of the ranch to visit a friend in town and got stuck in traffic. Zachary can't fire you for that."

"You're not just a guest," Hildie said, shooting a glance at Tina's growing abdomen. "You're carrying his child. Zachary takes that seriously. He would guard you and the baby with his life. He's still suffering—" Hildie broke off and shook her head.

"I know," Tina said. "My friend Keely told me all about it. It's actually the reason I went to visit her."

Hildie stared at her in shock. "You came to town so you could snoop about Zachary's past?"

"It wasn't snooping," Tina said, feeling her indignation shoot up to heat her cheeks. "He knew everything about me, yet neither you nor he would answer my questions. I sensed there was something, but never this." Tina felt another dip of nausea in her stomach when she thought of what Zachary had been through. His loss had been devastating.

Hildie was silent for a long moment as she inched the car forward. Then she sighed. "Well, maybe it's better that you know. Now you'll understand why he acts the way he does. That doesn't change the fact that Zachary Logan is going to fire me. If it weren't bad enough that I drove you into town without telling him, I forgot my cell phone. He'll be worrying himself sick when he gets in and nobody's at home."

"If he were that worried, he would call me, wouldn't he?" Tina asked as she pulled her cell phone from her purse. She'd put it on silent as soon as she'd sent a text to her brother this morning, preferring to ignore another rant. Glancing at it, she saw three calls from Zach's phone. "Oh, no," she murmured.

Hildie shot a quick glance at her. "What do you mean *oh, no?*"

"Nothing I can't handle. I'll go ahead and give Zach a call just in case he's within range," Tina said, dialing his number.

The phone rang half a ring before she heard his voice. "Tina," he said.

The sound of the rough growl of his voice grabbed at her.

"Yes, it's me. I thought I should give you a call since we're stuck in traffic."

"We? Does this mean you're with Hildie?"

"Yes, I tried to talk her into letting me borrow her car, but she was insistent that she take me where I needed to go."

"And where was that?" he asked with an edge to his voice.

"Just to visit Keely." A vehicle rammed into the back of Hildie's car, jerking Tina from the impact. "Oh!"

Hildie started swearing.

"Tina, what the hell—" Zach began.

The vehicle rammed them again. "Oh, what's the bloody fool thinking?" Tina demanded, momentarily forgetting her decorum as she braced her hands against the dash.

"Tina," Zach repeated. "What is going on?"

"We had—you Americans call it a fender bender," she said, her heart still racing. "Lord, I hope he's done," she said to Hildie, whose face had turned white. "Are you okay, Hildie?"

"I'm fine," the older woman said, putting the car in Park. "Where are the cops when you need them? Damn lunatic. I'll teach him a lesson he won't forget."

Tina watched in shock as Hildie got out of the car and marched to the pickup truck behind them. The housekeeper immediately began pointing at her car and appeared to be giving the driver a complete verbal thrashing. "You weren't stretching the truth when you said Hildie had fought off a bear, were you?"

"Tina, are you okay?" Zach asked. "Is Hildie okay?"

"I'm fine. Hildie's fine, but I feel sorry for the man who ran into us."

An hour later, Zach pulled his SUV into the body shop where Hildie's car had been towed. His gaze flew to Tina and even though she'd assured him that she was fine, he felt a sliver of relief as she appeared to hover over Hildie, who sat on a bench outside the body shop. The rain had stopped over a half hour ago, and the hot Texas sun had dried everything in sight.

Tina glanced up and gave him a royal wave. Hildie covered her eyes. Zach wasn't sure what to do about Hildie. He gave and demanded complete loyalty from his employees, and Hildie had stepped over the line. She knew he didn't want Tina setting foot outside the ranch without his knowledge since he was still trying to protect Tina from the paparazzi.

He got out of his car and Hildie immediately approached him with regret written on her face. "I know. There's no excuse."

"Oh, this is ridiculous," Tina said. "Hildie's convinced you're going to fire her. I know you wouldn't do a thing like that. All she did was drive me to visit a friend."

Feeling like a bubbling cauldron of emotions, Zach ground his teeth. "Hildie, Tina," he said as he opened the front and back passenger side doors. "Get in the car. I'll be back as soon as I talk with the body shop manager."

Zach took care of business with the body shop and returned to the car. "I'm taking both of you to a doctor to make sure you're okay."

"That's unnecessary," Tina said.

"I'm fine," Hildie said.

"Not optional," Zach said. "Injuries sometimes show up later. It's better to know sooner rather than later."

"It was no more than a jerky ride at an amusement park," Tina protested.

"Which is one more thing you should avoid during pregnancy," he said, feeling his temper build. "I can't believe the two of you did this without telling me."

"I'm sorry," Hildie said. "There's no excuse."

"It's not as if Hildie took me out for a tour of bars or skydiving. She just took me to see Keely. I asked if I could borrow her car."

"Oh, my God," he said, envisioning Tina in Dallas traffic. "Don't even think about it. You don't have enough experience."

"I have a driver's license. I have experience. I've driven in the jungle, for Pete's sake," she said.

"But not on the right hand side of the road," he said.

"When Hildie refused, I told her I would just have to rent a car."

Zach bit back an oath. "Have you forgotten that you're trying to avoid the paparazzi? How do you plan to do that if you're renting cars and lunching in Dallas?"

"Keely had takeout," Tina said. "Tell the truth. If Hildie or I had told you we planned to visit Keely today, what would you have said?"

"I would have suggested that you wait until I could take you," he said. "Maybe sometime next week."

"Exactly," Tina said. "You have a very busy schedule and you can't be expected to be at my beck and call. I also cannot be expected to stay at home all day every day."

Even though he knew Tina was right, his gut told him different. His gut told him to keep her locked in his house. Safe from the paparazzi. Safe from an accident. Safe, period.

He was beginning to realize that he couldn't control this woman. His best bet was maintaining influence. His goal was marriage. "We can talk about this later," he said. "Right now, I'm taking you to the doctor."

Several moments of blessed silence later, he pulled in front of the doctor's office and helped both Tina and Hildie out of the car. Tina held back while Hildie walked toward the office. She stepped in front of Zach and lifted her chin, her eyes blazing in defiance. "I think you should know that if you fire Hildie, I'll leave the ranch."

He stared at her in astonishment. The woman was determined to drive him crazy. He swallowed a dozen oaths then slowly nodded. "Fine. Hildie stays as long as you stay."

Tina's jaw dropped at how quickly he'd turned her threat into his favor, but she cleared her throat and quickly collected her composure, the way any good princess would. "I didn't mean it exactly that way."

"Are you saying you're willing for Hildie to be fired?" he asked.

"Of course not," Tina said. "But I won't be manipulated into staying at your ranch against my will."

"Are you staying against your will now?" he asked.

She hesitated a half-breath. "No, but I don't know how I'll feel. How you'll feel. I can't promise to stay at your ranch forever."

He nodded. "How about a year?" he countered.

She blinked. "A year?"

"You stay a year in exchange for Hildie's unlimited employment," he bargained, buying time. More than anything, time was what he needed.

Biting her lip, Tina looked away.

Zach had noticed that she knew how to control how she revealed emotion, so he could tell she was conflicted. "A year isn't that long. It will give you time to have the baby and for you and I to know each other."

She glanced up and searched his eyes. He wondered what she was looking for. "Six months. That will be a month after the baby is due. That's all I'll promise."

Zach felt a rush of triumph. He'd just bought himself half a year.

* * *

It didn't take long for Tina to suspect that she'd been duped. She'd been so eager to protect Hildie that she hadn't considered that Zach would use her stance against her. After the doctor cleared both her and the baby and Hildie, they returned to the ranch.

"Tell Hildie she won't be fired. I can't bear her cowering. It's so out of character," she said to Zach just before they entered the house.

His lips twitched. "I told her when the doctor was seeing you."

"Oh," she said and met his gaze, thinking about all she'd learned about him today. She'd just given herself a six-month sentence with the most desirable, yet impossible, man alive. She wondered how she would survive it.

"I'm tired. Baby and I need some sleep," she said and stepped through the doorway. Two steps later, she felt Zach's hand clasp hers.

"After you have something to eat and drink," he said.

"I'm not really hungry," she said.

"Then Hildie can just fix you a sandwich," he said.

"Hildie is more worn out than I am," she said. "If you insist, I'll fix my own."

He swore under his breath. "Damn, you're a handful. I will fix your sandwich. Turkey or ham?"

"Are you sure you know how?" she countered, unable to resist the opportunity to jab at him.

His eyes lit with a combination of sensuality and irritation. "Yeah, I know how to make a sandwich. Does your highly-ness prefer mustard or mayonnaise? Pickles or naked?"

The word naked caught her off guard and a flash of his gorgeous, naked muscular body ricocheted through her brain. She blinked to push it away. "Dill pickles and I'd love sparkling water if you have some," she said, trying, but not at all succeeding in pretending he was just a member of staff. With the heat he generated inside her, she was going to have to find some way of coping with him.

For the next two days, Zachary left her alone. Tina wasn't sure if she liked that or not. She was torn between taking the time to figure out what she should do after her six months with Zach and being bored out of her mind. She wasn't accustomed to so much *rest*. Heaven help her, she began to understand the concept of being bored to death.

Of course, negotiating a field trip with Hildie was out of the question. Zach's housekeeper had been unfailingly polite since the accident but refused to chat about anything more than the weather.

Late at night after she'd had nearly zero conversation with a human being throughout the day, she decided to take a bath and listen to music and perhaps talk to her sister Fredericka, who was in England at the moment.

Making sure the bathwater was the perfect temperature, she sank into the tub and sipped a glass of sparkling water and pretended it was champagne. She turned on the music of a French rock band and closed her eyes.

Tina toyed with the spigot with her toes, noting that she could use a pedicure. When she'd lived at the palace, a mani-pedi had been a weekly ritual she'd regarded as a waste of time. Her schedule had been packed with appearances. Now, her schedule was one big yawn.

Sighing, she glanced down at her wet, slowly burgeoning belly and smiled. "Will your eyes be blue or green?" she whispered. "Are you a girl or a boy? I'll love you either way," she promised. "Your father will love you either way, too."

Taking a deep breath, she leaned back against the pillow to support her head and focused on the pleasure of the bath instead of the turmoil of her life.

Minutes or seconds later, the door to her bath opened and Zachary stepped inside, his body rigid with alarm. "Tina," he said then made a face. "Why didn't you answer the door?"

Automatically trying to cover herself, she lifted one hand to her breast and one hand much lower after she pulled an earphone loose. "What are you doing? Haven't you heard of knocking?"

"I did, but you didn't answer," he said, his gaze traveling over her body from head to toe and back again. "You didn't answer, so I thought I'd better check on you in case you drowned."

Feeling her nipples grow tighter from the cool air and his stare, she frowned at him. "I didn't drown, so you can leave."

He didn't move fast enough for her, so she picked up her wet rag and tossed it at him. He caught it, of course. "Out! Get out. You don't speak to me for days then you wait until I'm naked and enjoying a bath."

The water dripped onto his shirt. "Are you saying you feel neglected?"

Furious beyond any concern for her nudity, she stood in the tub and screamed. "Get out."

The next morning when she awakened, she found a note pushed under her door. "Oh, goody. Another trip to the obstetrician," she muttered as she picked it up. Despite her crabby mood, she opened the note instead of ripping it into a thousand pieces.

Dinner out tonight. 6:30 pm. Wear a dress.—Zach

Oh, that silver-tongued devil, she thought. How could she possibly resist such charm and seduction? She considered refusing. For at least two whole minutes. Then she realized she had nothing else to do. Dinner with Zachary. She had ten hours to choose her dress.

* * *

Zach wore a white shirt and a pair of black slacks. It was strange as hell, but he felt a little nervous about taking Tina to dinner. Despite the fact that they'd shared a bed way too many nights ago and despite the fact that she'd been staying in his home for weeks now, she was still a princess. More important, she was the mother of his child and he needed to win her over.

Considering the fact that his heart was closed to any chance of romance and love, he was facing a tough proposition. Glancing down, he hoped the bouquet of flowers would help.

He heard her first foot on the top step and glanced upward. Her legs were bare, creamy and curvy. She wore a turquoise flowing dress that hinted at her curves and pregnancy, but didn't give all her secrets away. Her hair fell like a silk curtain to her shoulders and her eyes held curiosity.

Curiosity was better than the fury he'd seen last night when she'd stood naked screaming at him. The visual of her wet, nude body would be stamped on his mind forever. It had taken two cold showers before he'd been able to pull his libido under control.

She kept reminding him that despite his missing heart, his sexual desire was alive and kicking. As she came to a stop beside him, he resisted the urge to ditch their dinner and persuade her to spend the night with him in his bed.

"You look good," he said in a voice that sounded rough to his own ears.

"Thank you," she said, her eyelids dropping to cover her eyes for a second. "So do you."

He felt a kick of arousal. She glanced up at him again and took the flowers he held in his hand. "Lovely flowers," she said softly and kissed his cheek. "Thank you."

Zach's gaze dipped to the creamy cleft of her cleavage and

he clenched his jaw. Every move she made reminded him of what he was missing by not having her in his bed. This entire evening was going to be one big pain in his groin.

Chapter Ten

The candlelight at their table for two flickered over Zachary's tanned complexion, reflecting against his white teeth and shirt. He seemed a little lighter tonight. He smiled more and laughed more. The low, husky sound was both contagious and seductive.

Except for the two of them, the small restaurant was deserted. "You still haven't told me how you managed to close down this place for this night just for you and me," she said. "That sounds like something only a king could do."

He lifted his eyebrows, but held her gaze. "I'm no king. This place is usually closed on this night of the week. I just called in a favor."

She narrowed her eyes at him, but not in an unfriendly way. "You seem to have quite a few favors you can call in."

Zach shrugged his shoulders, drawing her attention to his strength again, not that it had ever left her mind. "One hand washes the other. One good turn deserves another," he said.

"Hmm," she said. "Is this a form of the Texas mafia?"

Zach laughed and the sound rippled through her. Underneath the surface of their light romantic evening, Tina was always aware of what she'd just learned about Zach. The pain and loss he'd suffered. The fact that he'd brought in a new obstetrician after his wife and baby had died. The way he'd protected her since the first moment they'd met. Yet, he had also made her feel like a woman instead of a royal title.

Every once in a while, he showed flashes of himself beneath the hard, tough surface. She wondered what it would take to get all the way in. She wondered if it was possible. She wondered if she could do it. Did she even want to?

"You may deny it, but in your way, you're a king of your own country with plenty of diplomatic connections. Or favors, as you call them," she said.

"I'm just a rancher and a businessman," he said.

She chuckled and gave the same response he'd given her a few times. "Uh-huh. And I'm Little Bo Peep."

"Give me a break. How can I impress a princess?"

Charmed, despite all her reservations and she had quite a few, she smiled. "You did that a long time ago," she said softly.

His eyes turned serious and he reached across the table to take her hand. "Is that true or are you giving the proper princess response?"

She rolled her eyes. "I haven't been proper with you since the first time I met you."

He rubbed her fingers sensually. "I always thought I was damn lucky that night even when I had no clue you were a princess."

Torn between seduction and a need for reassurance, she lowered her gaze to their entwined hands. "What was so

great about me? It's not as if I'm beauty queen material—"
She broke off when his fingers covered her lips. The sensation made her heart skip over itself. The intensity in his gaze squeezed her chest so tight she could barely breathe.

He shook his head and pulled his fingers away from her mouth. "You're the strangest combination of a woman I've ever met. Mysterious, voluptuous, too sexy for your own good and mine too. And sweet. Irresistible as hell."

His response was so honest and baffled that she had to believe him. He made her feel powerful and vulnerable at the same time.

The nearly invisible waiter appeared beside their table at that moment. She tried to pull back her hand, but he wouldn't let her.

"Yes," he said to the waiter.

The waiter cleared his throat. "Dessert if you wish," he said nodding to both of them. "Chocolate mousse or apple pie à la mode."

Zach looked at her. "Ladies' choice."

"Easy," she said. "Chocolate mousse, but I'd like to share."

Zach lifted his mouth in a half-grin. "Good idea."

Within moments, the waiter returned with the mousse and two spoons. Zach put one aside. "We only need one. Should I try it first to make sure there's nothing wrong with it? Didn't the royals used to do that? Have some poor schmuck taste the food in case it was poisoned?"

She rolled her eyes at him and took the spoon. "I'm sure it's fine, especially since you called in a favor." She dipped the spoon into the mousse and lifted it to her mouth, sliding it onto her tongue. Closing her eyes, she moaned. "Now, that is good. Almost as good as my favorite restaurant in Paris."

She finally opened her eyes and met his gaze, which was filled with heat and sensual determination.

"You know, that comment could make a man want to make you forget about Paris," he said.

Her heart skittered again. "That could be a pretty big challenge. Paris is an amazing city." She dipped the spoon into the mousse and lifted it to his mouth.

He reached out and wrapped his hand around hers as she guided it to his lips. His tongue slipped out to scoop up the mousse. She watched his strong throat work down the silky confection.

"Give me a chance and see what happens," he said.

After dinner, he led her to the SUV. Before he helped her inside, however, he pushed her back against his car and lowered his head. Her stomach felt as if she were riding a jerky ride in an amusement park.

He pressed his mouth against hers and she welcomed the plush sensation and forbidden taste of his lips. He was better than the chocolate mousse they'd shared. More tempting, more…everything…

She clung to him, craving more of him. Could she possibly find the man he'd become before his loss?

"Let's go home," he muttered against her mouth. "We can figure it out there."

Plunged into a sensual, Zachary-ruled daze, she nodded. "Yes, I think that's a good idea."

Zach helped her into his car and drove back to the ranch. The drive was silent, giving her plenty of opportunity to come to her senses, but for some reason, her rational side had decided to play hooky as Keely had described to Tina years ago.

Zach pulled his SUV inside the garage and cut the engine. He looked at her and her heartbeat immediately picked up. Lowering his head, he pressed his mouth against hers again. "Come to my room."

She sucked in a quick, sharp breath, but her mind remained muddy and seduced. "Are you sure this is—"

"I'm sure," he said, cutting through her uncertainty. "Are you?"

"Ohh," she said, resting her forehead against his, searching for sanity.

"Ohh isn't good enough. I need a *yes*."

He wasn't going to let her abdicate her responsibility or her response. She couldn't help but admire him for that. He was making her play fair for the both of them.

"Yes," she managed. "Yes, I want to be with you."

One second passed and he led her upstairs. He swept her away so quickly, she wasn't sure if her feet touched the stairs. She barely took two more breaths and she felt herself falling onto his bed, staring up at him.

"That was fast," she whispered.

"Think of it as three months of foreplay," he said, unbuttoning his shirt and unzipping his pants.

She watched him in wonder, his gleaming, broad bare chest and flat abdomen. She felt the wicked urge to press her cheek against his strong belly. He stole the opportunity from her as he followed her down and stripped off her clothes between kisses.

She felt the heat inside her build to an unbearable height as she arched beneath him, straining to feel every inch of his strong, naked body against her.

Taking her mouth in a French kiss, he slid his hand down her shoulder then lower to her swollen breast. As he stroked her, she felt a corresponding tug in her nether regions.

He pushed his thigh between her legs as a prelude to his possession, and something inside her ripped loose. Need, primitive and consuming, suddenly roared through her like a forest fire.

Unable to remain still, she pressed and rolled her body

against his. He let out a low visceral moan that vibrated through their mouths.

"Careful," he muttered, slipping one of his hands over her hip. "I'm trying to keep it slow."

She didn't want it slow. She wanted it fast and furious and now. Her head was a cloud of sexual need. "Now," she whispered.

He made another low sound, one of agonizing frustration. The controlled power in his moan gave her a tiny bit of mental satisfaction. He slipped one of his hands down between her thighs and stroked her where she was wet and swollen for him.

When she didn't think she could bear the anticipation one second longer, he pushed her legs apart and thrust inside her. Staring into his eyes, she realized she'd never felt so fully possessed by a man in her life. The connection she felt went so much deeper than sex. She also realized that she wanted to possess him in the same way.

Moving in an age-old rhythm, he thrust and she arched. Her climax took her by surprise. One heartbeat later, he stiffened as his release rippled through him, echoing throughout her.

The sound of their breaths mingled in the air, the same as their bodies. He covered her with his strength, bearing his weight on his forearms to protect her. He took a few more breaths and rolled to her side.

Her heart still pounding, she turned her head to look at him, wondering if he was feeling half as much as she was. Wondering if it was more than physical for him.

The back of his opposite forearm covered his face, shielding his expression from her, and an odd vulnerability made her stomach dip.

Biting the inside of her lip, she scooted her hand over to

his and slid her fingers through his. His arm immediately dropped and he met her gaze as he rolled to his side again.

"You okay?" he asked, lifting his fingers to touch her hair. The tenderness in the gesture gave her hope.

She nodded.

He stroked her hair and she closed her eyes, her emotions pulling her in a dozen different directions. Although she was physically satisfied, her heart felt heavy. She felt shockingly vulnerable.

Taking a deep breath, she felt as if she needed to get herself back together, to cover up her emotional nakedness. She opened her eyes, but didn't look at him. "I should probably go," she said and started to get up.

Zach squeezed her hand. "No," he said in a dark, urgent voice. "Stay."

Tina did stay in Zach's bedroom, sleeping every night with him for the next two weeks. Every night she hoped for some kind of breakthrough and saw signs of it in the little things. His arm curling around her body and pulling her against him before they fell asleep. His laughter when she was too sleepy to open her eyes early in the morning. The way he stroked her hair every night and brushed a secret kiss on the top of her head.

She hoped it meant that he was beginning to feel something for her, because heaven help her, she was feeling something for Zach she'd never dreamed.

"Picnic," she told him through sleep-heavy eyes as he was getting ready to leave one morning.

"Picnic?" he echoed.

She nodded, struggling to open her droopy eyes. "I want you to take me for a picnic to your favorite place."

He paused a half-beat. "Okay. Next week."

"Today or tomorrow," she corrected.

"I have things scheduled," he said.

"Schedule me," she said, lifting up on her forearms.

He met her gaze and his lips lifted in a crooked half-grin. "Is that a royal decree?"

"Would that help?" she asked.

He chuckled. "Not necessary. Tomorrow. My workers will mock me for taking so much time out in the middle of the day."

"And you'll tell them I'm worth it," she said, brushing her hair from her face.

He stepped to the side of the bed and slid his fingers through the back of her hair and gave her a hard kiss. "Damn, you make me want to climb back in bed with you. Have a good day and stay out of trouble."

During the day when Zach was gone, Tina feared she would be bored out of her mind. That day, she approached Hildie, begging for a distraction. "Please let me help. I need to do something, or I'll go crazy."

"You need to rest," Hildie said. "You're pregnant and—"

"Oh, rubbish," Tina said, irritated. "Pregnant women have been productive for ages. I can't just sit here like a hen on an egg."

Hildie twisted her mouth as if she were trying not to smile. "Maybe you should order some books on child rearing."

"Maybe I should take skydiving lessons," Tina countered.

Hildie twitched but lifted her chin. "I won't fall for your threats again. I learned my lesson the first time when you nearly got me fired."

"Oh, you wouldn't have been fired," Tina said. "And I took care of it in case Zach lost his mind and did something impulsive."

Hildie froze. "Took care of what?"

Tina realized she'd slipped and shrugged. "It was nothing. Heavens, can you please give me something to do? I need to feel productive."

"You could always muck out a stall," Hildie's niece Eve said dryly as she cruised into the kitchen.

Tina tossed the young woman an amused grin. "You almost tempt me. How are the darlings?" she asked, speaking of Zach's horses.

"Good," she said. "The colt still needs a little extra work, but that's going to be tough to do with me gone most of the time. The price of corporate success," she said and made a face as she pushed a glass into the door of the refrigerator to get some water.

"Are you saying you wish you could be doing something different?" Tina asked.

"Of course not," Hildie said. "Eve works for a big company that pays her a big salary with nice benefits."

Eve lifted an eyebrow at Tina. "Of course. What Hildie said."

"I would think there would be lots of ranchers who would need your kind of expertise," Tina ventured.

Eve shrugged. "Probably, but matching my current pay would be nearly impossible."

Tina tucked that fact into her mind for future contemplation. After all, since she was gestating, she had plenty of time to think.

"We have the charity drive for the children's wing at the hospital coming up in a few weeks, though, so that will keep all of us busy. We do a little carnival for children and donate the money we make to the hospital," Eve said, taking a long drink from her glass.

"Charity drive?" Tina echoed.

Hildie scowled at Eve. "You need to be careful what you say in front of her."

Tina frowned. "Why? I'm not a child." She narrowed her eyes. "Has Zachary told you to shield me from what's going on in the community? If so, he and I will definitely have a discussion."

"He didn't use the word shield," Hildie said.

Tina began to stew. "I'll just bet he didn't. And did he threaten your job? Because if he did, Zachary and I made a deal about your job. As long as I stay at the ranch until one month after the baby is born, he can't fire you. Period. Not that he would have in the first place," she added.

Hildie blinked at her. "You made a deal for me?"

"Of course I did," Tina said. "I practically forced you to drive me to Dallas."

Hildie met her gaze and her eyes grew shiny with unshed tears. "I don't know what to say. Zachary has always been good to me, but you don't know me that well and you stood up for me anyway."

Tina was flattered. Hildie wasn't one to give faint praise. "It was nothing," she said. "Now can someone fill me in on the details of this charity event? After all, charity events are my specialty."

Eve exchanged a look with Hildie. "Can you imagine how much people would pay to have lunch with a princess?"

"Children?" Hildie asked.

Eve shook her head. "Adults. Think about it. You're digging weeds next to your neighbor's fence and casually mention, 'I had lunch with a princess last weekend.'"

Hildie grimaced. "Zachary will kill us."

"Maybe," Eve said. "But he can't fire you."

Excitement raced through Tina. Now, she had a project, a purpose.

The following day, however, she had a totally different

purpose. As Zachary drove his truck to the spot for the picnic, she experimented with how she would ask him the questions that had been burning inside her. It was long past time for them to discuss some very important issues, and she hoped with every inch of her that he would be both receptive and responsive. If she'd believed in crossed fingers and toes, she would be doing both.

Zachary pulled to a stop next to a weeping willow tree and a small pond. There was a small stand of grass and some bluebonnets stubbornly showing their gorgeous blossoms on the edge of the idyllic mound.

"It's beautiful," she said.

He nodded. "I stole away to this place when I was a kid as much as I could in the summertime."

"I can see why. Shade, water and grass. What more could a young boy want?"

"A swing," he said. "I would swing on that tree and go flying into the pond. Sometimes all three of us, my brother, sister and I, would play hooky on a hot day and come here."

"Good times," she said, watching his eyes light with happy memories. "Maybe they can come back sometime soon."

His happiness seemed to fade. "Maybe," he said and grabbed the picnic basket and blanket. "Let's eat."

Zach spread out the blanket and Tina unloaded the picnic basket, quelling her nerves about how he might respond to her. Hildie had prepared delicious club sandwiches, fruit and cookies for their mini feast.

"Hildie's an excellent cook," Tina said.

Zach nodded as he ate his sandwich. "She's worked for my family for a long time."

"You don't know how lucky you are. At the palace, each person receives one assignment." She shot him a dry smile. "Except for the royals. We do everything."

"Do you still like taking a break?" he asked. "I want you to feel like you can take a break."

"I can only do that for a while before I get, well, bored. I need to feel productive," she said.

He set down his sandwich. "Does that mean you want to return to your country?" he asked.

His stark expression took her off guard. "No," she said quickly. "As much as I love my country and people, I think it's time for some of my other family members to contribute. In the meantime, though, I need to be productive wherever I am. Here," she said, meeting his gaze.

He nodded thoughtfully. "I can understand that. We'll just need to coordinate it with avoiding the paparazzi. I don't want you to have to deal with that hassle."

"You've been quite successful," she said. "Perhaps the palace could take lessons from you."

He chuckled. "Amazing what a couple of cowboys with shotguns can do."

She nodded, her mind still heavy with the subject that continuously hovered in her mind. "There is something I've wanted to ask you about."

"Ask," he said and took another bite of his sandwich.

She took a sip of water to dampen her suddenly dry mouth then took a calming breath. "I know you were married and that you lost your wife and baby. I'm so sorry for all you've suffered. I'm so sorry for your loss."

His face closed up and his eyes turned hard. "I don't discuss that," he said. "With anyone."

Chapter Eleven

Disappointed by Zach's abrupt response, Tina stared into his closed gaze. She had hoped that their physical intimacy had mirrored a growing emotional intimacy. "I just want you to feel like you can talk with me about it. After all, I'm having your child and—"

Zach shook his head. "I'm not going to talk about it. If you want to push the conversation, we may as well leave. But I had something else I wanted to discuss with you and I think both of us would like that subject much better," he said.

She could tell by the set of his jaw that she wasn't going to get anywhere talking about his wife and child. The knowledge frustrated her, but she didn't want to ruin their afternoon. That didn't stop her from hoping he would open up to her some other time.

"Okay," she relented. "What did you want to discuss?"

His gaze relaxed slightly. "In a little bit. Let's enjoy the lunch, first."

"That was a tease," she said, her curiosity piqued.

"How do you like it here?" he asked.

"It's taking some getting used to," she said. "The isolation can be both good and bad. It's nice going out and not feeling like I'm being watched by everyone and my photograph isn't being taken every other second. I still find it amazing that you've been able to keep the paparazzi away."

"I'm not obligated to allow anyone to see you," he pointed out. "My job is to protect you. As far as the palace PR is concerned, they can take a royal leap."

She chuckled, imagining the response of the advisers and her brother. She couldn't deny, however, how refreshing it was to have someone so protective of her. Although the palace security force had always been quite protective, they were sworn to protect the monarchy. Zach wasn't sworn to protect anyone. He just did it.

"Do you think this is a good place to raise a child?" he asked.

She nodded slowly. "Yes, for the most part. As much as I have felt suffocated by my duties during the last several years, I would, however, like my child to be familiar with my country and family. I think the sense of history from both the mother and father is important."

"So you would want to visit Chantaine?" he said.

"I'm still figuring it out, but yes, I think so. If my brother allows it," she added.

"Allows it?" he echoed in displeasure. "How in hell could he disallow it? You're a princess. What could he do to you?"

"He's the ruling monarch. He could strip me of my title if he wanted," she said. "Stefan is very angry and although I know he loves and respects me, he doesn't understand my actions. He doesn't understand how I could turn my back on my duties."

"What about your own choices? Your own life?" he asked.

She smiled. "You sound like an American. Lots of choices. Not as many when you're born into royalty."

"Are you afraid of having your title taken away?"

"I'm not so concerned about the title, but the idea of losing all connection with my family hurts me," she said. "But I have to focus on my child's future. As grateful as I am for all the opportunities I've had, I don't want my child growing up in an environment where obligation is primary. I hope my child will learn to appreciate the rewards of service and I'll do what I can to make that happen. But I do want my child to have more choices."

He leaned toward her and took her hands in his. "You don't need to be afraid. I would always take care of you whether you have a title or not."

The expression of dedication on his face turned her heart to butter. "Thank you. That means a lot. When I realized I was pregnant, though, I knew the person I most needed to rely on was myself."

He shook his head. "But you know you don't need to do this alone."

"I know," she said.

"That's part of what I wanted to discuss with you," he said. "We've touched on the subject before, but I think it's time to take the next step." He reached into his pocket and pulled out a jeweler's box.

Tina gaped at Zach as a sense of unreality fell over her. He opened the jeweler's box to reveal a beautiful diamond ring.

"I'll always be true to you. I'll always take care of you and our child. Through thick and thin, bad and good, I know how to stick with it. I can't think of any greater gift you and

I can give our child than to be married, to be husband and wife. Marry me, Tina."

Her heart stopped, along with her breath. "You mentioned this before, but..." She stared at the diamond ring and searched his face. Tina had received proposals before. Two, in fact, but she'd known beyond a shadow of a doubt that she couldn't accept them. The very idea of binding herself to either of those men forever had made her physically ill.

Zach, however, was a totally different man. Her feelings for him were totally different. She slept with him every night and she was carrying his child.

"I don't know what to say," she said. "I didn't expect this. Not today."

"You're growing," he said and slid his hand over her belly. "Our baby is growing. You and I know we want each other and we want what's right for our child. Marriages have been built on much more shaky ground than that. It's the right thing to do."

His last sentence turned Tina cold inside. She'd spent her life doing what she was told because *it was the right thing to do.* The first time she hadn't done the right thing, she'd experienced passion beyond her imagination. She's also gotten pregnant. If anything, she was more determined than ever not to make such a huge decision simply because it was the right thing to do.

She shook her head. "I can't," she finally managed.

Zach looked at her in surprise. "Why?"

She sighed. "There's got to be more. I need for us to be—" She broke off, feeling self-conscious and vulnerable.

"Be what?" he demanded. "We're lovers. We're committed."

"We may be lovers," she said. "But we're not in love."

He pulled back and a cynical expression crossed his face.

"Even though you're a princess, I never would have tagged you as a woman who believed in fairy tales."

She frowned at him. "Who says love is a fairy tale? There are plenty of people who find love," she said. "Look at Keely and Brent."

"That's rare," he said. "And just because they feel in love now, doesn't mean it will last."

"You sound so jaded," she said. "I wouldn't have expected that of you."

"It's not jaded. It's just practical," he said. "If you base decisions on emotion, you'll end up in a big mess."

"If that's true, then what about that first night we shared together? Do you consider that we're in a big mess?"

"I wouldn't call it a big mess, but it's not optimal."

She frowned, studying him, trying to figure out where his attitude originated. "Is this about your own marriage? Was your relationship a disappointment? Or did you love her so much you can't love again?"

His eyes turned cold again. "I told you I don't discuss my marriage with anyone. We may as well go back to the house."

Her stomach twisting in knots, Tina refused to let him see how upset she was. "I agree," she said.

Zach went into Dallas to work the next day. He needed a break from the princess in his ranch. He successfully plunged himself into work until his brother took him out to a bar.

The loud strains of a country rock band played in the background as Zach drank his second Jack and Coke.

Daniel clicked his double shot of bourbon against Zach's glass. "To success," he said. "All our businesses are doing great."

"Yeah," Zach said. "To success. Thanks for staying on top of the in-town biz. I owe you."

"I'll let you pay me back over time. How are things with the princess?"

"She's okay," Zach said. He took another swig of his drink. "Just making things difficult. I asked her to marry me."

Daniel swiveled on his bar stool and stared at Zach. "And?"

"You know she's pregnant. It's the right thing," Zach said.

"I guess she said no," Daniel said.

"Pretty much," Zach said. "She wants to rehash everything that happened with Jenny and the baby."

Daniel cringed. "Oh. That would suck."

"You're telling me," Zach said and took another long swallow from his drink. "Why isn't a proposal, a ring and a commitment forever enough?"

"Women," Daniel said, shaking his head. "I'll never really understand them. Like I'm trying to take care of—" He broke off abruptly as if he'd thought better of stating his thoughts aloud.

"Take care of what?" Zach asked.

Daniel shook his head. "Nothing that's gonna make any difference."

"Sounds like a woman," Zach said.

Daniel looked at him and grinned. "Could be right."

"Does this have anything to do with the property you're thinking about buying that's close to mine?"

"Don't ask. Don't tell," Daniel said.

"Whoa," Zach said, his mind working double time. "I'm trying to think what could possibly draw you back to Logan County." He paused, searching his memory. "The only thing that comes to mind is Chloe Martin. She has a kid. Not sure what's going on with her husband..."

Daniel's face turned dark. "Like I said, don't ask. Don't tell."

"Is her husband alive?" Zach asked

"No," Daniel said. "Next subject."

Understanding how much pain a woman could cause a man, Zach cut his brother some slack and changed the subject as he'd requested. "I like that singer Trace Adkins. Do you?"

"Yeah," Daniel said. "I think the man has suffered."

"Most of us have," Zach said.

A blonde stepped between them at the bar and smiled at both of them. "How ya doin', boys? Wanna buy me a drink?"

Zach briefly thought of another time in his life when he was free and could hit the sheets with a woman for a night of mindless satisfaction. Even though the woman bared the tops of her breasts and smiled with sensual invitation, he felt nothing.

"Sorry. I could buy you a drink, but that's where it would end," he said.

"Me too," Daniel said.

The woman gave a wry smile. "Thanks for being honest. I hope I find someone like you."

Zach watched her walk away as did Daniel.

"We are in a bad, bad way," Daniel said.

"Yeah," Zach said. "It's just plain sad."

"So how you gonna work it out with the princess?" Daniel asked.

"No idea," Zach said. "Maybe another Jack and Coke will tell me."

Daniel laughed. "Good luck with that."

Zach took a taxi to his Dallas apartment and stripped out of his clothes, then sank onto his bed alone. His brain was swimming. His arms were reaching for Tina.

She'd filled his nights and dreams, making him forget his pain with her body and warmth. Tonight he instinctively reached for her, but she wasn't there. She'd become more than a warm body to him. She'd warmed his cold soul and heart. But he still couldn't let her in. Letting her in could destroy him. How could he possibly remain strong if he let down his guard to her?

His gut twisted and he felt more empty than ever. Swearing to himself, he wondered how he could keep her without becoming vulnerable....

Tina stayed awake until well past midnight. Zach didn't return, she noticed. She slept in the guest bed because she couldn't imagine returning to his bed. She didn't know if he would want her. She didn't know if she could give herself as freely as she had in the past.

She resented Zach's reluctance to discuss his loss with her. At the same time, she understood it. Sometimes loss was private, but she also knew that keeping silent could cause wounds to fester. When her father had died, she was given instructions from palace PR how to properly discuss her grief. The same with her mother, who had died years before.

Be strong, she'd been told. And Tina had done her best, but now, years later, she wanted and needed a more authentic relationship, one where they didn't hide important things from each other.

For the next several weeks, Zach spent most of his time working in Dallas. He called Tina every day to check on her, but their conversations felt stilted. Although she'd focused on helping with the children's hospital charity event, Tina couldn't help feeling cranky about the wide gulf that separated them. He might as well be in Timbuktu.

After finishing another conversation with Zach, Tina returned to the kitchen to continue counting the receipts from the charity event with Hildie and her niece.

Several moments passed while she concentrated on the pile in front of her.

"You're quiet," Eve said. "Anything wrong?"

Tina sighed. "Nothing more than usual," she muttered.

Eve widened her eyes. "Then what's the usual? The lunch with a princess event was a huge hit. We made a lot of money."

She shrugged. "It's not the charity event. It's the useless conversation I have every day with Zachary. Same question, same answer. Done in two minutes. Even after my latest ultrasound showed I'm carrying a girl, he didn't seem to have much to say. If he's going to spend all his time in Dallas, it makes me wonder why I'm staying here."

"Zachary has always divided his time between the ranch and the businesses in Dallas," Hildie said. "It's not unusual for him to be gone a month at a time if business is going well. I was surprised he managed to stay here as long as he did when you first arrived. He's usually in town at least one day every two weeks. Often more."

Tina nodded, but she wasn't at all sure Zachary's motivation didn't stem from their argument the day before he left. "The timing for this trip seems a bit coincidental."

"How's that?" Eve asked, stretching a rubber band around her receipts and setting them aside.

"We had a discussion the day before he went to Dallas. It didn't go well," Tina said.

Hildie refilled each of their cups with hot tea. "I can't imagine what kind of discussion would bother Zachary that much. Unless it concerned Jenny and the baby."

Tina couldn't quite conceal a small grimace.

"Oh, no, you didn't," Hildie said.

"I think it's important that we're open about this," Tina said. "He clearly has strong feelings about the fact that I'm pregnant. I mean, he doesn't love me, but he asked me to marry him and—"

Eve's jaw dropped. "He asked you to marry him? Why didn't you tell us you two were engaged?"

"Because we're not," Tina said. "I turned him down."

Both women stared at her in shock.

"You turned down a proposal from Zachary Logan? The father of your child?" Hildie asked.

"He doesn't love me," Tina said.

Hildie snorted. "That would change. With the right people, love will grow."

"No wonder he's camping out in Dallas," Eve said.

"You act as if this is all my fault," Tina said. "All I wanted was for Zach to share a little about his relationship with his wife with me. Just a few words."

"Easier to rip out his spleen," Eve said.

"Or his liver," Hildie added.

Frustrated by the accusatory looks from the women, Tina met their gazes one at a time. "His proposal included the words. *It's the right thing to do.*"

"Well, it is," Hildie said.

Eve paused. "Yeah, but I can see your point. If you're looking for hearts and flowers, it was missing in a big way."

"If you're looking for hearts and flowers from Zachary Logan, then you're looking in the wrong place. Zachary is more solid than all that. He's the kind of man who will stay true."

"I wasn't wanting hearts and flowers. I wanted to know that he wasn't marrying me just because I was pregnant." She folded her hands together. "I wanted this proposal to be different. I've received proposals from other men where our marriage would have been a kind of barter. A trade of my title and position for something they could offer my country.

With Zach, I just wanted to believe love between us was really possible."

"I can't blame you for that," Eve said.

Hildie's mouth was set in a frown for a long, silent moment. "Well, if you're serious about this love thing, then you better realize it's gotta go both ways. Maybe you could do a little more on your end, if you get my drift, your highlyness."

Chapter Twelve

That night, Tina tossed and turned. The suggestion that she should extend herself more to Zach irritated her. After all, she was here on his ranch in Texas instead of Paris, Italy or even her own country. That should mean something.

Besides, after their picnic disaster and Zachary's subsequent disappearance, he should come to her. He was the one who'd been unreasonable. And for goodness sake, she was a Devereaux. A Devereaux didn't go chasing after ranchers.

For one flicker of a moment, she thought how horrible that last thought would sound if she said it aloud. Tina groaned. She sounded just like a princess. Oh, heaven help her and everyone who encountered her in her current mood.

She would do something, she told herself. She didn't know what, and she didn't know how, but she would do something. Tomorrow, she resolved. It was after 2:00 a.m. and she and the baby needed their rest.

Dragging herself out of bed the next morning, she stayed

in her room while she sipped a cup of tea and wished it were coffee. Her head felt as if it were full of mud. She stared out her window at the changing colors of the landscape of Zach's ranch. Although the temperatures were still warm, the vivid greens of summer were beginning to fade with the changing of the season.

Feeling a kick from the baby, she smiled and put her hand over her belly. She had always been protective of her family and people in need, but she'd never felt such a consuming urge to shield anyone as she did her baby.

A tap on the door interrupted her thoughts. "Yes?" she called.

"It's Hildie," the housekeeper said and opened the door. "What can I fix you for breakfast?"

"I'm not very hungry. I can toast myself an English muffin," she said.

Hildie lifted her eyebrows in disapproval. "The baby may want more than that to eat."

"The baby's fine," Tina said. "She's doing her morning kickboxing. Would you like to feel her?"

Hildie looked hesitant, then quickly moved toward her. She extended her hand and Tina drew it against her abdomen. The baby gave several quick kicks and Hildie's eyes widened. "She's a little pistol, isn't she?"

Tina nodded and laughed. "My thoughts exactly."

Hildie sat gingerly on the chair beside Tina, her hand still resting on Tina's belly. Longing darkened her gaze. "I planned on having children, but when my husband died after six years of marriage—" She shook her head.

"And you never met another man who interested you enough to give him a chance?" Tina asked.

Hildie shook her head and lifted her lips in a sad smile. "Chet was my one and only. I was a lucky woman to have him every day that I had him. I just wish I still had a piece of him by having a child, but it wasn't meant to be." She removed her hand from Tina's abdomen. "Feels like she quieted down a little now."

"I never dreamed how amazing it would feel to have a baby growing inside me," Tina said. "Yes, there are definitely some discomforts, but it really is a miracle. Speaking of miracles, I have been thinking about what you said to me last night. At first, I was offended, but I've decided you may be right. Perhaps I should make an overture toward Zachary."

"I'm glad to hear that," Hildie said with a firm nod. "Shows you're a good, strong woman."

"Thank you," Tina said. "In order to make my overture, however, I'm going to need your assistance."

Hildie immediately looked doubtful. "My assistance?" she echoed and immediately shook her head. "If you think I'm going to take you anywhere without notifying Zachary, then you're wrong. Princess or no, you got me in big trouble last time. Zachary made it perfectly clear that—"

Tina lifted her hand. "I want to surprise Zachary at his Dallas apartment. I'd like to take him a meal. We can prepare the meal tomorrow and you can drive me to his apartment where I will surprise him when he arrives home from work. Now tell me," Tina said, putting her hand over Hildie's. "What could possibly go wrong with that plan?"

After Hildie showed Tina her secret recipe for Zachary's favorite pot roast with onions, potatoes and carrots, Hildie and Tina made a few quick stops along the way to Zachary's apartment so that she would arrive about an hour before Zachary was expected to leave the office.

Tina adjusted the shades on the windows and rearranged the small bouquet of flowers as she waited for him. She felt a crazy combination of emotions as she fluttered around the apartment where she and Zach had shared that first passionate night together.

She wondered how he would feel about her unexpected visit. A home-cooked meal would push aside some of his reservations she hoped, and glanced at the clock again. Hildie had given her precise instructions for reheating the roast. According to the time, she could begin the process in eight minutes.

Too edgy to relax, she poured herself a glass of water and walked through the small apartment again. Although the living space appeared comfortable, it was so generic-looking that she wondered how Zach could possibly stand to spend so much time here without adding just a few of his own belongings to make it feel more welcoming.

"It's been a rough week for both of us," Daniel said. "Let's go out for a steak."

"I don't know," Zach said. He'd been wrestling with memories and regrets all day. "I thought I would just grab a burger and watch some mindless TV tonight."

Daniel made a face. "That's what you do every night. C'mon. We can go to Hooligan's Bar and drown our sorrows together."

"We just acquired a new company for nearly nothing. What do you need to drown your sorrows about?" Zach asked.

Daniel scowled. "I don't wanna talk about it. Just like you don't wanna talk about it."

"I don't know if this is a good idea. That place can get wild on Friday nights."

"Stop arguing and come on. It's not like you have any other plans," Daniel said.

Tina put the pot roast on at precisely the time Hildie had instructed, added the dinner rolls to the oven, then put salad into bowls. Although she had rarely set a table, she knew how. Glancing at the clock, she sat at the small dinette table and wished she had brought something to read or her laptop.

Instead, she checked her text messages and voice mails. Her sisters were finally starting to settle into performing their official duties, although they often complained to Tina.

During the last few months, Tina had shared tips on making their tasks easier, but she truly believed that dividing the assignments was what made the job less of a beast.

Her brother, however, was still the same beast he'd always been. He'd gone through a threatening stage with Tina. Then he'd turned silent, refusing to speak to her. As much as Tina loved her brother, his silence had been far easier to bear.

She wished he would find a woman, or at least a mistress. Surely that would ease some of his…frustration.

The timer went off, signaling that dinner was ready. Tina glanced at the clock and frowned. No sign of Zach. He must be staying a little late, she decided, and turned off the oven. Hopefully, he would be home soon.

Minutes turned into hours and Tina didn't know what to do. This was supposed to be a surprise, so she didn't want to call him. She considered calling Hildie but didn't want to drag the housekeeper into the situation any further. Hildie had been a nervous wreck during the entire drive from the ranch.

Sighing, she decided to wait. She turned on the television. Knowing Zachary, there was a perfect explanation. And it wasn't as if he'd known she would be here. She just hoped she didn't ruin the roast before he arrived.

Hours later, Tina awakened to the sound of the door opening and footsteps. She rose from her cramped position on the sofa in front of the television. She wasn't sure when she'd fallen asleep.

"Zach?"

Zach came to a dead stop in the hallway just outside the den. "Tina?" he asked, rubbing his face as if he couldn't believe his eyes.

Relief shot through her and she walked toward him. She noticed his hair and clothes looked disheveled. "Yes, I was hoping to surprise—" She broke off as she caught a whiff of his breath then something else that immediately made her stomach knot with suspicion. "Where have you been?"

Zach raked his hand through his mussed hair. "Daniel insisted on taking me out to dinner. He said I needed to get out. How long have you been here? Why didn't you tell me you were coming?"

She noticed his words were just slightly slurred and frowned. She'd been waiting here like the good little wife while he'd been out drinking. "You smell like liquor," she said, darts of fury poking through her like spikes.

"Yeah, I had a few too many. I took a taxi home," he said. "I'm sorry I wasn't here when—"

"You also smell like cheap perfume," she said, identifying the other odor he was *wearing*.

Zach lifted his hand. "That's not my fault. Daniel was flirting with these two women and they kept trying to get me to dance. One of the women was really pushy and sat down on my lap. The only way I could get her away was by leaving."

Tina was so upset she could hardly breathe. "*Sitting on your lap,*" she said, barely swallowing the urge to shriek. "Is this what you've been doing every night? No wonder you haven't returned to the ranch. You've been too busy having all your *fun.*"

"No," he said, but she couldn't stand to hear any more excuses. She felt like a total fool for waiting for him while he'd been out drinking and letting pushy women sit on his lap.

"I need to go," she said more to herself than him. She couldn't stand one more minute in his presence. "A cab," she said, walking to the sofa to grab her purse. "I'll get a cab."

"Wait," he said, wrapping his hand around her arm. "Don't leave. Please."

Delaying the urge to shake his hand away from her, she took a small breath. That was all she could manage. "Why?" she demanded. "If you had decided to surprise me with my favorite dinner and I had come home smelling of liquor and another man's cologne, what would you do?"

He clenched his jaw. "After I killed the guy?" he asked.

She rolled her eyes and tugged at her arm. "Let me go. This was a huge mistake. I shouldn't have done this. If this is who you really are, then I've made more than one mistake," she said, her voice breaking.

"It's not," he insisted and stood in front of the door, blocking her way. "This isn't who I really am. You know that. You've been around me."

"But tonight—"

Pain sliced through his eyes before he closed them. "Tonight is—" He gave a rough groan as if the words were being wrenched from deep inside him. "This is the date Jenny and the baby died."

Zachary stared into Tina's eyes and immediately regretted his words.

Sympathy darkened her green gaze and he swore. "I'm so—"

"Damn it, don't feel sorry for me."

She blinked then her brow furrowed. "What am I supposed to say? Too bad. Chin up. Or you must have done something horrible for such a horrible thing to happen to you. Or why didn't you prevent it? Because, after all, you have the power to prevent all tragedy. Correct?"

This time he was taken aback by what she'd said. Due to

the excessive quantity of whiskey he'd consumed, his mind wasn't moving as fast as usual. Somehow she'd hit on every one of his worst fears. *Bad things happen to bad people. He should have done more to prevent...*

"Go take a shower," she said. "You'll feel better."

He hesitated, still holding her in his sights, afraid she might vanish in a puff of air. She could be a hallucination. "You'll stay?" he asked.

She nodded. "For now."

"You won't leave without telling me first," he said. "And the deal is I have to be cognizant. Because after I take a shower and fall into bed, I won't be conscious for a while."

Her lips twitched. "I agree to the deal," she said. "Now go take a shower."

He pushed away from the door but stopped before he passed her. "Sure you don't want to join me?"

Her eyes rounded in surprise. "In the shower?"

"And in bed," he said, wanting to feel her soft body against his. She could make him forget for a while. She already had.

She chuckled. "Go."

Walking to the bathroom, he shucked his clothes and turned on the shower. If he were smart, he would give himself a cold shower as punishment for indulging in his secret pity party tonight, but at the moment, he couldn't summon his masochistic demons. They were usually close by. With gallows humor, he wondered if Tina had scared them away.

Washing the evening from his skin with soap, he allowed the hot water to slide over him. After an extra moment of the soothing sensation, he climbed out of the tub and dried himself off. Still blinking against the bright light of the bathroom, he brushed his teeth, wrapped the towel around his waist and headed for his bed.

His mind was still muddled and seeing Tina reminded

him of everything he'd been missing since he'd left the ranch. Even half-lit he knew that he wouldn't be in his finest sexual form tonight.

Dropping the towel on the rug beside his bed, he climbed into bed and sighed.

"There's water on your nightstand if you get thirsty," Tina said from the open doorway, the light spilling around her in a backlight that resembled a halo.

Zach wondered again if she was some kind of apparition. Glancing at the nightstand, he saw a cup of water. He took a quick gulp. "Thanks. G'night," he said and surrendered to his weariness.

Crossing her arms over her belly, Tina was full of emotions as she stared into the darkened room. She had traded her crazy life at the palace for an uncertain future with a man chasing his own demons. He was, however, the father of her child and he'd granted her a glimpse of his humanity for just a few moments tonight.

That authenticity was what she'd been craving, what she felt she needed as much as water, as oxygen. Vacillating about what she should do now, she heard Zach snore softly. She shrugged and went to get her nightgown from her overnight bag. In for a penny. In for a euro.

The next morning, Zach awakened as the sun skimmed over his closed eyelids. His senses came to life slowly. He squinted then quickly closed his eyes against the light. His head throbbed unforgivingly and his throat was so dry he felt as if a troop of soldiers had stomped through it.

He groaned and rolled away from the sun, his hand encountering softness. Stretching his fingertips, he felt silky hair. He skimmed his fingers lower and felt skin that reminded him of velvet. Lower, he felt a silky strip of fabric.

"Good morning," Tina whispered, and her voice brought him into full awareness. She was in bed with him. He'd dreamed of this too many times to name.

He forced his eyes open to make sure he wasn't dreaming. His head still hammering, he took in the sight of her with her hair tousled over her green eyes, her cheeks flushed with sleep, her gown dipping low to reveal her lush cleavage.

"Morning," he said. "I can think of ten things I'd like to do to you right now, but the jackhammer in my head isn't going to let me, damn it," he muttered.

She gave a low laugh and pulled him against her for a sweet hug that was over way too quickly. He felt her roll away from him.

Wait, he wanted to say, but that damned hammer prevented him.

"Let me get you an aspirin," she said. "Go ahead and take a sip of water. I'll fix you some toast."

His stomach rolled at the prospect. "I don't want anything to eat."

"Just a bite or two," she said. "Trust me."

He leaned his head back and took some mind-clearing breaths. This was bad. Very bad. He didn't want Tina seeing him like this. He should have sent her home last night.

He heard her moving around but couldn't summon the strength to roar at her to tell her to leave. He felt like a frog paralyzed in preparation for dissection for a high school Biology lab.

"Here. Take this," she said, nudging him gently.

Shifting upward, he accepted the aspirin and water. He took a few bites of the toast and more sips of water.

"This sucks," he muttered. "I've been thinking about you every damn night and every damn morning. Now, I feel like something the cat dragged in."

She bit her lip as if she were trying to keep from laughing. "Rest. You'll feel better later."

Resisting sleep for at least three moments, he couldn't resist the call...of the pillow.

It must have been centuries later when Zach awakened to the smell of coffee. Climbing up from the depths of sleep, he struggled to open his eyes. He inhaled the scent, drawing it deep inside him, craving the jump-start of caffeine.

Rolling out of bed, he walked toward the smell of it, rubbing his eyes. His gaze traveled, then landed on Tina.

She stared at him in response, her gaze briefly lowered to his groin then rising upward. He glanced down, noting his nakedness.

"I hope there's a cup left of that coffee or I'm going to have to go out for some," he said.

Tina quickly poured a cup, brought it to him and pushed it into his hand, her gaze focused firmly on his face.

He took a long drink followed by another, then another. His head began to clear and he met her gaze. "Wanna go back to bed?"

Chapter Thirteen

Tina felt as if she should throw a dish towel over him. Oh, no, that wouldn't be big enough, she thought. A towel, she thought. Or a blanket.

"How about some more toast?" she countered.

Zach sighed and sucked down the rest of his cup of coffee. He held the empty cup out for her and she quickly refilled it.

She cleared her throat, determined not to look below his well-muscled chest. "Would you like a robe?"

He sipped his coffee and sighed again. "Give me a minute," he said and turned around, treating her to a view of his gorgeous backside as he returned to his bedroom. A moment later, he returned wearing a pair of jeans and an unbuttoned shirt.

He sat down at the dinette table and watched her through hooded eyes. "Toast sounds good," he said.

She served him four slices, then scrambled eggs. Cooking

wasn't Tina's forte, but she could manage a few things. She pushed two more slices of toast in front of him and watched him quickly consume them.

Still gazing at her, he raked his hand through his hair. "I don't remember as much as I should about last night," he said. "But I do remember you being here when I got back from dinner."

"Late, late dinner," she couldn't resist adding.

"Yeah," he said. "I stayed later than I should."

"Because it was the anniversary of your wife and baby's death," she said.

Her words stabbed him. He took a quick breath. "Yeah."

His gaze met hers. He didn't want to talk about it. He didn't say it aloud, but his expression yelled it.

"Hildie and I made a pot roast. She said it was your favorite. I reheated it just before I expected you to arrive home. I'm sorry to report that the pot roast may no longer be edible."

His lips twitched. "The toast and eggs were good."

"You would have had roast if you hadn't walked in smelling like liquor and cheap perfume," she said, still smarting over how long she'd waited for him.

"A woman sat on my lap without invitation. I left as soon as I could and grabbed a cab. The liquor was my brother's idea."

"I'm not sure I like your brother," she said.

"He's a nice enough guy," Zach said. "Just needs some direction." He hesitated a half-beat. "What made you come to the apartment to surprise me?"

She shook her head. "It's complicated. It stemmed from a discussion with Hildie. I haven't decided if it was a big mistake or not."

"What was your goal?" he asked.

"What do you mean?"

He shrugged, pouring himself another cup of coffee. "Did

you meet your goal? That's how you decide if it was a mistake or not."

She felt a surge of self-consciousness, but his gaze challenged her. She bit the inside of her lip because he wouldn't be able to see that. "I wanted to reach out to you. I was trying to make our relationship more two-way. I realized I hadn't extended myself much."

He shrugged his beautiful, muscular shoulders. "Then I would say you succeeded."

Her heart leapt at the hungry expression in his gaze.

"You wanna sneak out for a while?" he asked.

"Where?"

He shrugged again. "Anywhere. Just out," he said.

Anticipation rushed through her and she nodded. "Yes. Let's go."

A half hour later, he pressed a ball cap over her head and planted her sunglasses over her nose. He crammed another ball cap over his own head.

"Disguise," he said. "I don't want the paparazzi after you."

"I'm pretty sure they won't recognize me," she muttered, trying not to think about her now-flat hair.

"That's the goal," he said and took her hand in his. "Let's go."

He drove to a farmer's market which featured everything from fresh fruit and vegetables to jewelry and scarves. The carnival atmosphere lifted Tina's spirits.

"I'd like a few of these scarves for the nursery," she said, fingering a few of the pink pashminas.

"What are you going to do with them?" he asked.

"Hang them on the wall," she said, visualizing the nursery. "I haven't thought much about it, but I guess we need to get started."

"Yeah," he said, and lowered his hand to her belly. "How's the little princess doing?"

Her heart twisted. "Getting bigger. I think she may be a gymnast."

His lips lifted. "Busy little girl?"

She nodded. "Yes. Maybe she'll do a somersault for you soon."

He placed his other hand over her abdomen, cradling her belly. The baby jumped and kicked.

His laser blue eyes widened. "She's on the move."

"Yes, she is," she said, feeling her own kick of delight. "She must know her daddy is holding her."

He sucked in a deep breath and lowered his mouth to hers. "I've missed you, Tina. Damn it, I've missed you."

In the middle of that farmer's market, Tina kissed him and didn't care who was watching.

Later that night, Zach looked at the over-cooked pot roast with Tina and shook his head. "Now, that's a damn shame," he said. "I haven't had a good pot roast since I was at the ranch."

Tina crossed her arms over her chest. "I followed Hildie's instructions to the letter," she said defensively.

"I know you did," he said. "It's okay. Just sad in a fast-food-for-a-month-diet way," he said, chuckling under his breath. He glanced at her and chucked his index finger under her chin. "Fair payback for a stupid night of indulgence."

Her gaze softened. "You had good reason," she said.

He shrugged, not wanting to go to that dark place again. "Should we bury it?"

"Let's call Hildie first," she said.

"I dunno. She's gonna want an explanation."

"We should call her," Tina said. "She may have a suggestion."

Zach suspected Hildie would grill them on why they hadn't eaten the roast the way she'd intended. "Go ahead and call."

Tina's face fell. "I was thinking you could call."

Zach shook his head. "I don't like to get into discussions with Hildie about cooking."

Tina narrowed her eyes. "You're scared of her."

Zach reared back. "I'm *not* scared of her."

Tina lifted an eyebrow. "Then why won't you call her?"

"You brought the roast," he said.

She met his gaze and lifted her chin. "I'm Princess Valentina. I suppose I can face down anyone or anything, heaven help me," she added and punched in Hildie's cell number.

An hour later, after a quick trip to the corner market, Zach and Tina were enjoying barbecued beef sandwiches.

"Hildie is a genius," Tina said. "I never would have thought of barbecue sandwiches."

"That's because you're not from Texas," he said, downing his second sandwich.

"But you've got to admit it was inventive to turn dried-out pot roast into juicy beef barbecue," she said.

He nodded. "Hildie is first-rate," he said.

"You wouldn't want to try to replace her," Tina said.

"Hell no. I've had neighbors try to steal her away," he said.

"How did you manage to keep her?" she asked.

"Good retirement, health care and dental program," he said. "Plus, I drive her to all her dental appointments because as I said before, dentists scare the hell out of her."

"Hmm," Tina said with a nod as she nibbled on her sandwich. "So, it would take a lot for you to fire her," she concluded.

"Fire her," he echoed and shook his head. "The only way

I would fire Hildie is if she was stealing from me and that would never happen."

"So, you wouldn't have fired her for driving me to Dallas. You accepted my trade of her employment for my staying here because you wouldn't have fired her anyway," she said.

Zach's last bit of BBQ hung midway in his throat. He coughed and swallowed hard, not liking the look on Tina's face. But he took the ruthless choice. "I accepted your trade because I would do anything to keep you here. Anything," he said.

"Why?"

"Because you and our baby are very important to me," he said.

Tina set down her sandwich. "I wouldn't wish our baby away," she said. "But I wonder if I would be anywhere near as important if I weren't pregnant."

Zach's gut twisted at the expression on her face. "You can't really ask that because everything would be different," he said. "But if you want the cleanest, most honest reaction, go back to that first night we had together. That will tell you the truth." He set down his second sandwich and covered her hands with his. She felt so soft and vulnerable, yet at the same time, strong. "I wanted you. You wanted me. We both tried to take the right road and that road still led us to each other."

She took a quick audible breath. "Maybe," she finally said.

He shook his head. "Not maybe. Definitely."

That night after a long hot shower, Tina joined Zach in his bed. She fought a sliver of nervousness and smoothed her fingers over her cotton nightgown.

Already showered, he glanced up at her from the newspaper spread over the comforter. His dark hair was just starting to dry and his laser blue eyes were hooded by his thick black eyelashes. He looked like a dark panther waiting to pounce.

"I think I want some water," she said and made a U-turn for the kitchen. Tina wondered if this was a good idea. Did she really want to get so close to Zach again? *Of course she did.* Did she really want to make herself vulnerable? She bit the inside of her lip. That answer wasn't so easy.

She stared at the tall glass of water and took a sip.

Strong arms wrapped around her. "You're okay," he said. "It's not like I can get you knocked up again."

She couldn't resist the laugh that bubbled all the way from her uterus. Tina was pretty sure the baby was laughing too. "Oh my goodness," she said, turning in his arms. "You're such a smooth talker. How can I possibly resist?"

His mouth lifted in a crooked, sexy half grin. "That's what I was counting on," he said and lifted her up in his arms.

The gesture stole her heart. "I'm going to give you a hernia," she said.

"No chance. You're a lightweight," he said and carried her to his bedroom.

"I hope you have good health insurance," she whispered, leaning her head against his. "A hernia is in your future."

He laughed and shook his head. "I've lifted a two-ton tractor before. In comparison, you're a feather."

She laughed, tossing her head back. "You're full of flattery. Or as you Americans say, full of bull."

He set her down on the bed and stared at her. She didn't know what she looked like, but the way he gazed at her made her feel beautiful. He skimmed his hands over her hair, spread out beside her head, then touched her jaw, throat and shoulders as if he wanted to touch every inch of her.

He lowered his hands to the swell of her abdomen and she

held her breath as he caressed her belly. "You have no idea how beautiful you are."

His gentle possessiveness was an affirmation instead of a threat. Unable to stand any barriers between them, she lifted her nightgown and tossed it aside. Then she pushed his boxers off his hips.

His eyes darkened with need. "How am I going to hold back?"

"Maybe I don't want you to hold back," she whispered, arching toward him.

He slid his hands over her bare breasts and sucked in a quick breath of arousal. She felt his hardness against her. The obvious evidence of his need took her to a different level than she'd ever experienced.

She dragged his head downward and pressed his mouth against hers. He made sexy sounds of want and need that echoed inside her.

Zach lowered his mouth to her breast and took her nipple into his mouth. She arched upward, craving the most intimate connection they could achieve.

He rubbed his hand over her tummy at the same time he gave her a deep French kiss. "You have no idea how sexy you are. You have no idea how much I want you."

"Show me," she whispered as he slid his hand between her thighs.

And he did.

With just a little coaxing from Zachary, Tina decided to stretch her visit to his Dallas apartment for a few extra days. She enjoyed taking walks with him. Always donning the baseball cap, sunglasses and loose clothing to keep herself well-disguised, she felt more impatient than ever with her brother's resistance to making a public announcement regarding her pregnancy. She suspected he was hoping she would abandon her relationship with Zach and return to Chantaine.

Even though he was appalled that she would have a baby out of wedlock, more than anything Stefan wanted Tina back in the country. He wanted her back in charge of the royal appearances so he didn't have to deal with her younger, more difficult sisters.

On Tuesday, Zach kissed her just before he left. "Remember. Don't go out without your cap and sunglasses."

"I won't," she said, flopping onto her back and staring at the ceiling as she saw another day of hat hair and frumpy clothes in her future. Zach's reason for keeping her on the down-low was different than her brother's reasons. Zach was totally focused on her safety and he didn't want her to get stampeded by the press or an eager group of curious onlookers.

Her mutually agreed-upon captivity was starting to grate on her. Although she didn't miss the frantic pace of her schedule before she'd gotten pregnant, she needed more. She needed more of a feeling of accomplishment. At the moment, on a more superficial note, she needed a few new articles of clothing. Tina had started calling the baby Kiki because she kicked so much. Little Kiki was growing bigger all the time, which meant *she* was growing bigger too.

Tina pushed herself upward and put together a plan. Taxi to the shopping district, buy some clothes, return to the apartment, perform a quick makeover, then order takeout from somewhere wonderful. Rubbing her palms together, she could hardly wait until the stores opened.

Kicking inside her, the baby must have felt her excitement as Tina made her secret shopping mission on the windy day. She bought a couple new bras, more panties, two long-sleeved blouses, a black cardigan and a green pullover sweater, a pair of those vile maternity pants and a black dress that almost made her look sexy.

Glancing at her cell phone, she winced at the time and knew she would need to rush to not only arrive home before Zach, but also re-do herself.

Her arms full of shopping bags, she stepped outside the department store. A gust of wind caught her cap and whipped it away. Swearing under her breath, she chased it, but it slipped through her fingers. She watched in futility as it whipped down the street.

Shrugging, she raked her fingers through her hair and looked for a cab. No one would recognize her. It wasn't as if she was wearing a tiara. If she could only get a bloody cab. This was when staff came in handy. She waved her hand for a few moments, then decided to return to the department store for help.

"Excuse me," she said, lifting her sunglasses to the top of her head as she spoke to the woman at the information desk. "Could you please help me get a cab?"

The woman tore her gaze from some sort of gossip magazine. "Oh, sure," she said and stared at Tina for a long moment. She glanced down at the magazine then back at Tina.

Tina felt a terrible sinking sensation.

"You're the princess," the woman yelled. "You're Princess Valentina and you're pregnant!"

Tina gave a smile that for her was more of a cringe. "Pleasure to meet you," she said in a low voice. "Now could you please help me get a cab?"

"Oh, of course, your Highness," the woman said, quickly standing. "Would you mind giving me an autograph? I've never met a real princess before."

"A pen?" Tina asked, desperate to escape. The information clerk immediately supplied one and the magazine.

Tina couldn't bring herself to sign a copy of the rag sheet that had ratted her out. "Perhaps a piece of your establishment's stationary?"

The woman blinked. "Oh, okay," she said and pulled out a notepad with the store's logo. "My name's Lola."

Using the careful penmanship she'd been taught at a young age, Tina wrote Lola's name and her own signature. "There," she said and smiled. "Now, about that cab?"

It seemed to take forever, but a cab finally appeared outside the doors of the department store. Just as Tina walked to the door, two men walked inside the store and approached her, one aiming a camera at her.

"Princess Valentina, the official word from the palace is that you're on a well-deserved sabbatical but that you will return to Chantaine soon."

"How do you do?" she said, going into royal mode despite her casual appearance. "I wish I could talk, but I'm in a bit of a hurry. Good day," she said and walked forward.

The two men stepped in front of her.

"Begging your pardon, Princess, but you're clearly—" The man paused, waving his hand vaguely in the direction of her belly.

Bloody hell, she was going to be in trouble from all ends. "Yes, you're right. My official statement is—" She paused a half beat and smiled. "I've swallowed a watermelon seed and look how she's grown."

"She," the reporter echoed. "A girl. Who's the father? Is it Zachary Logan?"

"I must go," she said. "Please step aside. I can tell you're a gentleman. Surely you would respect a woman who has swallowed a watermelon seed."

The reporter smiled. "Let her go, Rick. We've got our scoop. Good luck, Princess. Don't be a stranger."

"Not bloody likely," she muttered under her breath as she

stepped into the cab. She wondered who was going to kill her first. Zach or her brother.

Zach pulled into the underground parking lot of his apartment and stepped into the elevator. Looking forward to seeing Tina, he leaned against the inner wall and cleared out a few text messages on his BlackBerry. Once he walked through his apartment door, he was leaving everything else behind.

The elevator doors whooshed open and Zach saw a commotion in the lobby. Several people rushed into the elevator.

"Glad I got out of that," one man said.

"Me too," the woman said, rubbing her forehead. "Did you hear what they were talking about? Something about a princess staying here."

Zach's gut knotted.

The man shook his head. "Now that could be one royal pain in the ass for the rest of us," he joked.

Sucking in a sharp breath of air, Zach bided his time until he could get off the elevator. What the hell had happened today? Was Tina okay? Had she escaped the melee downstairs? He glanced at his phone again and there were no messages from her.

The elevator finally arrived at his floor. Walking onto his floor, he held his breath, wondering if the press would be waiting outside his apartment door. A sliver of relief shot through him when he didn't see a soul. He moved quickly to his apartment, unlocked the door and stepped inside. He immediately locked the deadbolt behind him.

Jazz music played in the background. A second later, Tina stepped into the hallway, wearing a black dress and heels. As soon as her gaze met his, she shot him a huge smile. Her eyes sparkled.

"Surprise. Italian food will be delivered within thirty minutes."

Distracted by how beautiful she looked, but not quite able to rid himself of the image of the crowd in the lobby. "You look great, but I'm not sure Italian is in our future. The apartment lobby's a madhouse. I don't know how it happened, but the press has found you."

Her smile fell. "Bloody hell. I should have known that reporter wouldn't let me off so easily."

Zach blinked. "Reporter?"

Tina smiled, but it looked more like a grimace. "I had a little surprise today when I went shopping."

"Tell me about it," he said, getting a bad feeling.

"Everything went fine until I decided to leave," she said. "It was windy. My cap flew off. I had to get help getting a cab. A reporter and a camera man appeared out of nowhere, the way they always do. It all went downhill from there."

"How much did you tell him?"

Her cell phone began to ring. Even he knew that particular ring tone. It was her brother.

"Oh, bloody hell," she whispered. "This could ruin our dinner."

Chapter Fourteen

"I guess I should answer it," Tina said, oozing reluctance as the phone went into its second cycle of ringing.

"Let me talk to him," Zach said.

Tina shook her head and walked toward her purse resting on the couch. "That's not a good idea. The two of you need a proper introduction first."

She picked up the phone and punched the send button. "Stefan, how are you?"

Zach could hear the man's voice from across the room.

"Yes, I guess the news may be out. I didn't expect you to hear so quickly," she said.

The man's loud voice continued.

"Yes, I realize the announcement wasn't optimal, but it was going to happen sometime," she said. "And I didn't exactly call it a pregnancy. My official explanation was that I swallowed a watermelon seed." She met Zach's gaze and shot him a mischievous smile.

He couldn't hold back a chuckle at the image of Tina making such a statement.

She suddenly frowned. "Of course, I'm not trying to make you look like a fool."

The distress on her face put all his protective instincts on alert. He moved closer to her and gestured for her to hand over the phone.

She shook her head and lifted her hand. "Stefan, I meant no disrespect. I was caught off guard and attempted to use humor to defuse the situation."

Refusing to allow her brother to berate her, he put his hand over hers. "Give me the phone, sweetheart," he said firmly.

She took a breath and surrendered the phone. Stefan was yelling. Zach counted to ten, twenty, thirty. Finally, even the crown prince decided he needed oxygen.

"Have you said enough for now?" Zach drawled.

He heard a harsh intake of breath and a muffled oath. "I was speaking to my sister," Stefan said. "I wish to speak to my sister."

"Not right now," Zach said. "You've more than had your say. She's in a delicate condition and she doesn't need to have anyone yelling at her."

"Who in hell do you think you are to keep me from my sister?" Stefan demanded.

"I'm the father of her child," Zach said. "My job is to protect her. You're a prince. Tell your PR people to handle this. You've got better things to do."

"I don't want her reputation besmirched," Stefan said.

"I appreciate that," Zach said. "I'll do everything to protect her and the baby."

Silence followed. "You realize now that the press knows where she is, it will be more difficult than ever to protect her. How do you plan to do that? I could send over her guard…."

"Not necessary," Zach said. "I'll be packing her up and taking her to the ranch no later than tomorrow morning, and I'll assign one of my men to watch over her when I'm not available."

"The palace would be a much better place for her. We're equipped to deal with crowds and publicity, and there's a physician available twenty-four hours a day."

"Tina is staying here," Zach said firmly.

"For now," Stefan said, and those two little words raised Zach's hackles.

He refused to rise to Stefan's dig. "I think we've covered the essentials. Feel free to call me if you need anything else."

"I'll call my sister directly if I need to talk to her," Stefan shot back.

"Just don't upset her. Bye now," he said.

"Wait," Stefan said, some of the imperious tone fading from his voice. "Is it really a girl?"

Zach smiled. "Yes, it's a girl, and she's a kicker."

"That must be why Tina calls her Kiki," Stefan said.

"How'd you know that?"

"From the news," Stefan retorted, not bothering to hide his displeasure.

Zach stifled a chuckle. "I'm glad we had this little discussion. Bye," he said and turned off the phone and handed it to Tina.

"You're technically supposed to wait until Stefan ends the conversation," she said.

"Yeah, well, he technically shouldn't act like such a jerk to you."

"He really is under a lot of pressure," she said. "Most people don't know it, but my father was ill for several years. The advisers insisted we keep it secret because many people would have considered Stefan too young." She sighed. "This is terrible to say, but I wish he would get married."

Zach lifted an eyebrow. "So you think marriage can solve his problems, but not yours?"

"*I* don't have his kind of problems." She glanced at her cell phone. "The food should be here by now."

"Like I told you, the delivery guy may need a special escort to get through that lobby."

Her eyebrows knitted together in frustration. "Maybe if I put on a cap and—"

"No way," he said.

"This is my last night here. I wanted it to be…special," she said.

Something inside him squeezed tight at her admission and he rolled some solutions through his mind. "Give me the number of the restaurant. I'll see what I can do."

It took a few calls, but Zach arranged to meet the delivery man in the underground parking garage. Taking the elevator all the way down, he adjusted his ball cap and sunglasses. He walked into the garage and spotted a vehicle with the name of the Italian restaurant and walked toward it, cash in hand.

"Thanks for meeting me down here," Zach said.

The young man glanced around nervously. "I tried to lose them—"

Three men stepped out of the shadows, one armed with a camera and bright light. Zach held his hand up to his eyes, squinting. "What the—"

"Mr. Zachary Logan, we're with the *Worldly News*. Tell us, are you the father of Princess Valentina's baby? Are you planning to get married? Is it true that you kidnapped her from France? And there have been rumors she's having twins—"

"Twins," Zach repeated in alarm. "Hell, no. And the rest is none of your business," he said and headed for the elevator.

The men stepped in front of him. "Mr. Logan—"

"You need to get out of my way. This garage is exclusively for the residents of this building. Do I need to call the cops?"

"That delivery driver isn't a resident of this building," one of the reporters said.

"He brought me Italian food. Did you bring me Italian food? No. Get out," he said and shoved them aside as he walked into the elevator.

His temper rising with each floor he passed, he was ready to growl when he arrived on his floor and entered his apartment.

"I don't see how you stand it," he said as he dumped the bags of food on the dining room table. "Damn bloodsuckers were waiting for me in the parking garage."

Alarm shot across Tina's face. "What bloodsuckers?"

"The press or pretend reporters. I had to threaten them before they would let me get back on the elevator, for Pete's sake."

Tina bit her lip. "This was what I was always afraid of. Your life is totally different from mine. I knew you would find the lack of privacy a terrible invasion. To some extent, it will never change. It's a bit worse now because I'm pregnant and unmarried and Stefan insisted on trying to keep it secret, but dealing with the press and being in the public eye will always be at least a part of my life."

"Not if you spend most of your time at my ranch," he said.

She gave a sad smile. "I won't hide out forever. Although it was time for me to not be the only royal making most of the public appearances, I'm not a hermit. I crave that feeling of accomplishment I get when I can be a part of helping."

"What about the accomplishment of raising our child?"

"That will be part of raising our child. I want our child to see the joy of helping others. She won't be able to do that if I stay locked up at the ranch."

Frustration trickled through him like acid. Although he could understand part of what she said, the idea of her or their baby being exposed to the dirty paws of the paparazzi on a regular basis made his stomach churn.

She moved closer to him and lifted her hand to his arm. "I understand that this is difficult for you. You weren't raised in a fish bowl. Do you remember when I told you that I hadn't planned to tell you that I was pregnant? This is why."

His gut twisted at her words. She made an important point that he didn't want to be true. She was from a different world, and her different world wasn't just going to go away. "I'll figure something out," he said and pulled her against him. "I'm good at that. Trust me."

Tina returned to the ranch and continued to gestate. She badgered Hildie until the housekeeper taught her how to cook some of Zach's favorite dishes. Zach visited every weekend, and she felt closer to him. Then he would seem to draw away from her. Tina suspected his conflicting feelings were related to his former wife and child. The knowledge made her feel helpless, but if Tina even hinted at bringing up the subject, Zach immediately shut down. Tina felt as if they weren't making any progress.

Thanksgiving passed and she became larger than she'd ever dreamed possible. Despite the fact that she grew tired more quickly, Tina organized a charity drive for local families—parents, grandparents and children. She was thrilled with the response. So often at Christmas, only children were remembered, but Tina wanted all ages to experience the happiness of Christmas even if it was only in a small way.

"You're doing too much," Hildie said as Tina helped the

housekeeper bake Christmas cookies on a Friday afternoon while a chicken dish simmered in a large Crock-Pot.

"I told you before. I can't just sit like a hen on an egg," Tina said.

"Humph. At least it's Friday. Maybe Zach will get you to calm down."

"It's not like I'm running a marathon," Tina said as she put another sheet of cookies into the oven.

Eve sighed and munched on a cookie. "This is a great break from my job."

"You have a good job," Hildie said. "Good salary. Good benefits."

"If only I didn't hate it," Eve muttered.

Hildie whipped around. "There are much worse situations you could be in, Missy. Plenty of people would love to have your job."

"I know," Eve said with more than a trace of guilt in her voice. "I work hard, Aunt Hildie. I just don't like it."

Hildie sighed and patted Eve on the shoulder. "You won't have to do it forever. Maybe you can find someone who will pay you good money to take care of their horses."

Eve smiled, unconvinced. "Yeah, and maybe I'll win the lottery next week."

"Don't be negative," Hildie said. "You weren't raised that way."

A knock sounded on the front door. "I bet one of the ranch hands smelled the cookies," Hildie said with a knowing grin. She put a few still-warm cookies on a plate and headed for the door. "I'll feed 'em and tell them to get back to work."

Lost in thought, Tina sprinkled green sugar on the cookies. The baby was kicking and her back ached. She wondered when Zach would arrive.

In her peripheral awareness, she heard the sound of a familiar male voice. She stopped mid-sprinkle and listened more closely. Her heart jumped. "Stefan," she called and ran to the foyer, which was filled with a royal entourage.

Her brother in all his tall, strong handsomeness gaped at her. "Valentina," he said. "Oh, my God. You look like you're ready to pop."

She laughed then flung herself at him and gave him a big hug. "I've got a few more weeks. What are you doing here?"

His smile dipped. "I haven't been satisfied with our communication lately. I've been concerned that your—" He cleared his throat and frowned. "Mr. Logan has been keeping you from the palace and me."

Tina shook her head. "Oh, no. Zach has been in Dallas lately. I've been in charge of a special Christmas sharing project and I can't deny I've been very tired at the end of the day. I told Bridget I couldn't do as many e-consultations, so I think she's felt a bit overwhelmed. You may need to hold Phillipa's feet to the fire a bit more."

Stefan sighed and shook his head. "There's just no one who can replace you."

She waggled her finger at him. "There you go, flattering me. You must be desperate."

"We've truly missed you," he said. "All of us. I insist you return. The palace physician is ready to oversee the delivery of your baby."

She bit the inside of her lip, feeling pulled in opposing directions. Seeing her brother again made her homesick for Chantaine. "We can talk about that later. You must be exhausted from the flight. Let's get something to drink for you. Something to eat." She turned to Hildie. "His Royal Highness, the Prince of Chantaine, this is Hildie Ferguson, CEO of domestic life at the ranch."

"My pleasure to meet you, Ms. Ferguson," Stefan said. "Thank you for your hospitality."

"It's my pleasure, your highlyness. Would you care for some tea or apple cider?"

Stefan's mouth twitched at *highlyness*. Although Tina had attempted to tell Hildie the correct way to address royalty, her suggestions had seemed to fall on deaf ears. "Cider, thank you, and please call me Mr. Devereaux. We are, after all, in America, not Chantaine."

Hildie nodded. "And you can call me Hildie. Please come into the dining room. Have a seat and make yourself at home," she said to Stefan and the two men standing with him. "All of you."

The men moved to the dining room. "I'll help with the cider," Tina said as she returned to the kitchen with Hildie.

"You'll do no such thing. You sit down and visit with your brother," Hildie said.

"Brother?" Eve echoed, peeking around the corner. "Is this the prig prince?" she whispered.

"Hush," Hildie said.

Tina couldn't quite swallow a chuckle. "He's not all bad," she said and returned to the dining room with a plate of cookies. "How is the road construction project going?" she asked as she sat down.

"We're making progress, more slowly than I like, but it's coming along," he said.

"And the development of new business you've been pursuing?"

"Not bad. Ericka's husband had decided to use Chantaine for some more of his films and he has spread the word among the film industry that we offer excellent terms. We're also in negotiations with a cruise ship company to become one of the stops on their itinerary."

"That's terrific news. More jobs, more exposure."

"But not too much," he said. "There's a balance we're determined to keep." He smiled. "This is part of what I've missed with you. Bridget and Phillipa couldn't care less about infrastructure unless it interrupts their trip to the beach."

Tina laughed. "Give them time. They've only been doing the job for about five months."

Stefan shot her a look of doubt. "I've never been one to rely on wishful—"

He broke off as Eve served apple cider, lifting his eyebrow at Tina as a demand for an introduction.

She caught herself thinking how much fun it would be to watch Stefan try to pull his royal attitude over on Eve. "His Royal Highness, this is Eve Jackson. She's Hildie's niece, and she's excellent with horses. They call her the horse whisperer."

He rose and extended his hand. "Really? My pleasure."

Eve met his gaze and Tina could almost swear she felt a crackle of static electricity shoot between them.

"Your royal highness," she said. "I've heard so much about you."

Tina swallowed over the urge to chuckle as Stefan shot her a quick glance. "Why do I have the feeling most of it wasn't good?"

"Please excuse me," Eve said, her voice neutral. "I really need to get back to the barn."

"Of course," he said then looked at Tina again. "Was that one of your staff? You know, I need a new person to work with my horses. Is she that good?"

"Yes, Eve's that good," Tina said and rolled the idea of Eve working for her brother around in her mind. "She would love the job," she said then reconsidered. "On second thought, I'm not sure she would be interested in working for you," Tina said.

He lifted his chin, clearly affronted. "Why not? I would pay an excellent salary."

"Eve is a very modern, liberated woman. I don't think she's the kind to bow to anyone."

"Hmm," he said, rubbing his finger over his bottom lip as he wore a thoughtful expression.

Hildie came into the room with a platter of mile-high sandwiches. "I fixed you a snack since we won't be having dinner for a few more hours."

Stefan blinked in surprise. "Thank you. I wasn't planning to eat—"

"Please do," Hildie said, folding her hands in front of her apron. "And your men can have a bite too."

As soon as Hildie left, Stefan turned back to Tina. "I'm quite serious about having you return to Chantaine. My private jet is waiting for us in a small, private airport not far from here. I know the trip will be long, but the staff will make you as comfortable as possible. As you know, there will be a nurse on board if you need any medical—"

Tina put her hand on her brother's arm. "Stefan, I can't do that. I promised Zachary I would stay here at least until one month after the baby is born. He will want to be a part of the baby's life and—"

"It's not as if you're married," he said. "Or you would even consider marrying him. There are many men more suitable—"

Tina's defenses flew to the roof. "Zachary has been very protective and considerate. I can already tell he'll be a wonderful father."

Stefan's eyes rounded in horror. "You're not considering marrying him? Tina, I haven't mentioned this yet, but this is the kind of thing that could make the advisers suggest you surrender your title."

She bit the inside of her lip. The idea of losing her title was less frightening to her than losing the affection of the people for whom she'd worked so hard. From the beginning of this pregnancy, though, she'd been faced with difficult choices. "I won't be pressured into making a decision for my child based on a title. Do what you have to do."

Hearing a loud noise at the front door, she broke off. "What—"

"Who disarmed my ranch hand? Where is Tina?"

Zach's voice roared through the house. Tina stared at her brother. "You disarmed one of Zach's men?"

Stefan shrugged his shoulders. "He wasn't hurt. My men merely relieved him of his shotgun and cell—"

Zach burst into the room with two men hanging off of him, his eyes blazing. "What's going on here?" he demanded as the two men in their chairs jumped in front of Stefan.

Tina cringed. This was not the way she'd wanted Zach and her brother to meet. She took a quick breath. "His Royal Highness, Prince of Chantaine, this is Zachary Logan."

"Why is he here?" Zach asked.

Stefan slowly rose. "I'm here to take my sister back to Chantaine where she belongs."

"Over my dead body."

"That can be arranged, but it would be messy."

Chapter Fifteen

"Get off my property," Zach said, his blood pounding through his veins. It was all he could do not to go after Stefan even though the prince's guards would likely kill him. "You're trespassing."

Tina touched his arm. "Zach, he's my brother."

He sucked in a deep breath. Nothing inside him softened even one millimeter. "He came to take you away."

"I told him I wouldn't go," she said in a low voice.

Something inside him eased just a fraction. He glanced at her. "Did you?"

She nodded. "Yes. Remember, he will be our daughter's uncle."

Zach couldn't say he was thrilled with the idea. After all, Stefan's goons had disarmed his man and left the poor guy tied up on the side of the road. He gave a grudging shrug. "We were doing okay before you arrived."

Stefan rose, his eyes glittering. "For a royal, okay is never enough."

Zach stuffed his hand in his pocket to keep from punching the superior expression off of Stefan's face.

"Later," Tina said to him, squeezing his arm.

Her tone calmed some part of him and he took a deep breath, searching for some common ground. "I'm glad to see how much you care for Tina. All of us have grown to care for her too. She's a remarkable woman."

He saw a twinge of hostility drain from Stefan's face. "Yes, she is. You're lucky to have enjoyed her presence all these months."

"We have," Zach said.

"The palace wishes her to return immediately," Stefan said.

Zach's stomach twisted into a square knot. "That's her choice," he said, knowing he was taking a risk even though she'd said she would stay.

Stefan frowned. "She insists she wants to stay, but I still believe we can provide better medical care for her and the baby. We can provide a more thorough education for the child. More protection from the public."

"You can't provide the baby's father," Zach said.

"There are other men—"

"That's enough." Zach felt his blood pressure rise. Two heartbeats later, he felt her squeeze his arm again. Her gaze told him other men couldn't replace him. He took another breath, calming himself.

"Would you like a tour of the ranch?" Tina asked her brother. "Zach has a stable of beautiful horses."

"You like horses?" Zach asked cautiously.

"Like is an understatement," Stefan said in a dry tone.

Over the next half hour, Zach showed Prince Stefan his horses. Even Stefan was impressed.

"They're beautiful and well-trained. Perhaps I should steal your horse whisperer away," Stefan said.

"I'm not sure Eve will fit into your budget," Zach said. "She has an executive salary with benefits."

"But not from you," Stefan said.

"No," Zach reluctantly admitted. "But I helped her through college, so we have a deal. She takes care of my horses that need some extra attention."

"How long would she be required to pay that debt?" Stefan asked.

Zach shot him a half grin. "As long as I say."

Stefan nodded. "A smart man. What are your plans for my sister?"

Zach sighed. "I'm doing my damndest to get her to marry me."

Stefan narrowed his eyes. "You are not who I would have chosen for her."

"If there's one thing I've learned about Tina, it's that she doesn't want someone else making this kind of choice for her. You. Or me," Zach said.

Stefan regarded him thoughtfully. "True. But Tina cannot fully turn her back on Chantaine. In one way or another, she will always be our princess. She will want to return."

"Marriage is a negotiation," Zach said.

"Ah, yes, you know that because of your previous marriage. Please accept my sympathies," he said.

"You had me investigated," Zach said.

"I wouldn't be a good brother or ruler if I hadn't," he said. "The views of your former wife's parents are unfortunate. Her death and your child's could not have been prevented."

"Nice of you to say so," Zach said, the discussion turning his stomach.

"Trust me. I wouldn't say that if I couldn't find a way to

twist the story against you to influence Tina to return with me today," Stefan said, his gaze ruthless.

"Always good to know who's got my back," Zach said.

"I look after Chantaine," Stefan said.

"I look after Tina and the baby," Zach returned.

After that, they returned to the house. Tina greeted them with an anxious expression. "How did it go?" she asked Zach, then turned to Stefan. "What did you think of his horses?"

"They are quite beautiful and well-behaved. I would like to talk to his trainer," Stefan said, cutting his eyes at Zach.

"Eve will turn you down flat," Zach said in a low voice.

"We'll see. In the meantime, Valentina, I must leave. Are you sure you won't join me?" Stefan asked.

Zach's gut twisted as she glanced at him then away. "I told you I can't go back right now," she said to Stefan. "But I'm so glad you visited. Seeing you made me realize all the more how much I've missed you and the rest of the family."

"Good," Stefan said and kissed his sister on both cheeks. "I brought a gift for the baby."

"Really?" Tina said in surprise. "What?"

He waved to one of his staff who hurried to the stretch limo in front of the house. Seconds later, the man appeared with a white box wrapped with a satin bow. He gave the box to Stefan, who presented it to Tina.

Tina beamed at her brother. "What is it?"

"Open it and find out," Stefan said, laughing.

Tina removed the top of the box and her face softened. "A flop-eared bunny. You remembered."

"You had one as a child, but one of the staff misplaced it," Stefan said. "I thought your little Kiki might like one too."

Tina dropped the box to the ground and threw her arms around her brother. "Thank you, Stefan. It has been so good to see you."

Her brother squeezed her tightly in return. "We miss you, Tina. Come back soon."

She drew back and Zach watched her draw in a deep breath. Her eyes were shiny with unshed tears. "Call me about road construction and infrastructure."

Stefan chuckled. "I'll do that." He turned aside and lifted his head toward Zach. "Take care of her, Zachary Logan."

"I will," Zach promised, and within seconds, Stefan and his entourage rode away.

Thank God.

As they watched the stretch limo disappear into the distance, Zach watched Tina swipe tears from her eyes as she hugged the pink flop-eared bunny to herself. "I didn't know bunnies were your favorite," he said.

She sniffled. "You didn't ask."

Well, hell, he thought. How was he supposed to know he should have asked?

"Anything else I should know?" he asked and slid his hand around her waist.

She gave a soft teary chuckle. "Oh, Zachary, that kind of stuff takes a lifetime."

"Dinner's ready," Hildie called from the doorway. "Oh, no. Did they leave already?"

"Yes, Stefan is gone," Tina said.

Hildie crossed her arms over her chest. "Well, that's a darned shame. I made a fresh apple pie."

"If you put some ice cream on it, I bet we can talk Tina into eating a slice," Zach said.

"I don't feel very hungry," Tina said.

"I bet Kiki would like a bit of that pie," he said.

She shot him a sideways glance. "Maybe."

He coaxed her into joining him for dinner. At first, she wouldn't eat a bite, but she gradually ate part of her meal.

"So what is it about flop-eared bunnies?" he asked.

She smiled and took another bite. "My uncle gave me one before I was even born. He's passed away since. But that flop-eared bunny was the first stuffed animal I remember. He was also the first I remember losing."

"He?" Zach echoed.

"I named him Erie because of his ears," she said, her gaze growing distant.

Zach frowned. "You don't talk about your mom much. Did the two of you get along?"

Tina shrugged. "We weren't very close. She gave birth to me, then had her duties. I had mine."

"That sounds a little cold," he said.

"We weren't close," she said. "After I went away to college, I realized I would want to have a different relationship with my children. Keely and her mom are so close, yet her mom gives her space."

"And your mom?" Zach asked.

"She bred heirs to the throne and made appearances. She became ill and her health quickly deteriorated when I was in college. She died my junior year. I graduated early, so I could go home and contribute to a sense of continuity and comfort."

"What about your father?" he asked.

"He died soon after, which put Stefan under the microscope," she said. "That's why we're close."

"He's lucky that you were there for him," he said.

She shrugged. "Maybe," she said and glanced away. "What about your sister? What is she like?"

"She's strong and independent. She's in Chicago. I haven't kept in touch like I should, but seeing you and Stefan makes me want to call her."

Tina met his gaze and slowly smiled. "Do that. You won't regret it. Invite her here for Christmas," she said and leaned her head against her hand as she studied him. "What about you? Any favorite stuffed animals from childhood?"

He racked his brain. "A hippopotamus," he finally said.

She laughed. "But they hurt people," she said.

"Not when they're fluffy and stuffed full of cotton with painted-on smiles," he countered.

"I guess that's true," she said and slid her hand in his. "Do you remember your favorite childhood song?"

"If you're happy and you know it, stomp your feet," he said. "I didn't have to sit down for it. What about you?"

"Frérè Jacques," she said. "My nanny sang it to me before I went to sleep."

"Oh, a night-night song," he said. "My father tried to sing a song about the moon and me. I don't remember the words."

"What about your mother?" she asked.

"She hugged me a lot," he said.

"Did you sing anything to the baby before—" She broke off and dipped her head. "Before he passed on?"

Zach frowned. "How did you know the baby was a boy?"

"I didn't," she said. "I just guessed."

He thought back to his time with Jenny and how erratic her behavior had become later into her pregnancy. After they'd married, he'd wondered about her dramatic high and low moods and how the pregnancy had seemed to accentuate them. When they'd learned she had a mental illness, he'd kept tabs on her several times a day…except that one day when he'd been tied up with a crisis. As soon as he'd learned Jenny was in trouble, he'd scrambled to take her to the E.R.

Zach had sped toward the hospital, but Jenny had bled out. By the time he'd arrived, the doctors had been unable to rouse her and the baby was dead.

He would never forget the helpless feeling he'd experienced speeding toward the hospital. Even now, it made him break into a cold sweat. The doctor had told him they couldn't have saved her even if she'd been in the hospital at the time of her crisis. She'd lost too much blood too quickly.

"Zach," Tina said. "Are you okay?"

"Yeah, I'm okay. Not great, but okay." He forced a smile. "Do Kiki and her mom want a bite of that apple pie?"

Tina paused as if she suspected he was remembering something painful. "I can't believe you're in the mood for apple pie."

"I'll take a bite if you will," he said. "You know, we haven't talked about names."

Surprise flitted across her face. "We haven't. You haven't been around very much."

"That will change," he said, lacing his fingers through hers.

"Starting when?" she asked.

"Now."

"Really? Why is that?" she asked.

"Last week, I told Daniel I wasn't coming back to the city until after the baby was born. I wanted to stay close," he said. "And because the damned cell phone isn't dependable, I bought some two-way radios. Old school, but they should work."

"So you'll be here for a while?" she asked, her gaze filled with a combination of relief and pleasure.

"Yeah," he said. "As long as you need me, Tina. Now about those names," he began.

"I've thought of a thousand," she confessed. "Stella, Mc-Kayla, Lucia, Camille, Delphine, Martina. Of course there will be more than one name to choose."

"I think one of her names should be Valentina," he said.

Her lips lifted in a soft smile. "Why is that?"

"Because she's a busy girl and that's partly a testament to her mother. On another subject, Hildie tells me you haven't ordered any baby furniture. Even I know we need to cross that off the list."

"I hadn't really figured out where to put her. I don't think I'll need much more than a bassinet to start, especially since I'm not sure how long—" She broke off and shrugged her shoulders.

Her uncertainty twisted something inside him. "What do you need to be sure?" he demanded, struggling with his impatience.

"This is one of those areas where you and I don't share the same opinion," she began.

"You don't share the opinion that we would be better parents together than apart?" he asked, rising from his chair.

"I didn't say that, but I have a lot of things to consider. I promised you I would stay for a month after the baby is born. Isn't that enough for now?"

"No, it isn't," he said. "I want us to get married. We can work out what you need to do about visiting Chantaine and your family, but I think you know deep down that you belong here with me."

She opened her mouth and her eyes deepened with an emotion that sliced through the steel vault around his frozen heart. That was what she wanted from him. His heart. What she didn't understand was that he'd lost the ability to give it three years ago.

He watched her pull back her emotions and close her mouth, whatever words she'd thought left unsaid. He felt the twist of the knife inside him again. The feeling always surprised him because he'd felt like he'd turned into a man who couldn't be reached.

Tina and Hildie wrapped donated gifts for the elderly. Tina shifted in her chair, feeling generally uncomfortable. She wasn't sleeping well and she wasn't sure about her future.

Despite the holiday music playing in the background, she felt a little cranky.

She tied a red ribbon around the tissue paper and reached for an indoor geranium kit and began to wrap it. "Do you think Zachary will ever be able to fall in love again?" she asked.

Silence followed as Hildie tied her own bow. "That's a tough one," she said. "He had such a hard time with Jenny. She wasn't who she thought she was."

"What do you mean?" Tina asked, searching Hildie's face.

"Jenny had problems. They seemed to get worse the further into her pregnancy," Hildie said, tying a firm bow.

"What kind of problems? Other than her pregnancy?"

Hildie sighed. "I really shouldn't be talking about this, but the girl had some kind of mental problems. I don't think Zach knew about it before they got married. After Jenny died, though, it seemed her parents knew something. They blamed Zach for not watching her more closely. They even demanded that she and the baby be buried somewhere other than the Logan family burial ground." Hildie shook her head. "Heaven knows he hovered over her night and day. After she got pregnant, she would leave the house in the middle of the night. We'd all panic and go searching to find her."

"Oh my goodness. I had no idea," Tina said, imagining how trying that must have been for all of them.

"Toward the end, Zach wouldn't go anywhere. She was about seven months along and started cramping and bleeding. We called Zach and he came right away. He took her to the hospital, but it was too late for Jenny. Too early for the baby. He blamed himself. The doctor said she had an undetected abruption. She started bleeding and didn't stop."

Hildie wrapped a bundle of sudoku books and tied a ribbon around the top. "You're nothing like her," she finally said.

"Is that good or bad?" Tina asked.

"Good," Hildie said. "But you have to realize what a terrible experience that was for a man like Zachary. He's a man who prides himself on fixing things, on taking care of people. In his mind, he failed in the worst way imaginable. Thank goodness you don't have mental problems," she said.

"Oh, I don't know," Tina said, absorbing the information Hildie had disclosed. "Depending on the day, all of us can feel a little off center, don't you think?"

Hildie met her gaze and gave a sassy smile. "Speak for yourself. I'm always on target."

"Show-off," Tina teased.

Hildie just grinned, but Tina's mind was spinning with what she'd just learned. Her heart ached even more for how Zach had suffered. Was he so scarred, however, that he would never be able to love again?

Chapter Sixteen

"Is there a reason we had to stop by the barn before going back to the ranch?" Tina called from Zach's SUV after she'd finished her latest appointment with the obstetrician. "I'm hungry."

"Eat your crackers," he said as he stalled for a little more time. Grinning to himself, he killed some time talking to his beauties in the barn while Tina waited in the car. It was for a good cause. She would ultimately be pleased.

Hearing her footsteps behind him, he wiped his grin off his face and looked busy.

"You hire people to take care of your horses. Why are you doing this?" she asked.

"I may hire people, but I still check on them. It's a good practice. And it's not as if Eve has had any spare time lately," he added.

"True," Tina said. "She's working crazy hours."

"And she hates it," Zach said.

"I wonder if my brother really would—"

Zach lifted his hand, finding the possibility untenable. Eve was the equivalent of his youngest sister. He didn't want to see her hurt. "Your brother is a bulldozer."

"You may be underestimating Eve. She's pretty strong," Tina said and sighed. "Can we please go now?"

Zach glanced at his watch. "Yeah, let me check the rest of the horses," he said and slowly walked through the rest of the barn. When he was certain he'd taken enough time, he returned to escort Tina to the car.

"Are you sure you're okay?" he asked. "You seem like you're out of breath a lot."

"The baby's riding high. That's what Hildie says. Causes indigestion and short breaths," she said, wobbling into her seat.

"Sorry about that," he said.

"If she was riding low, I'd have to run to the powder room all the time," she said with a shrug. "It's just part of pregnancy."

"Would you ever want to do it again?" he asked, holding the door open.

She scrunched up her face. "I'd prefer to reserve judgment on that decision. This isn't the best time to ask."

"When is the best time?" he asked.

"Maybe a year after the baby is born," she said.

He chuckled and nodded. "I'll make a note of it," he said and closed the door.

Climbing into the driver's side of the SUV, he took his time starting the engine and putting it into gear.

"Is there something wrong with the car?" she asked.

"No," he said. "Why?"

"Because you're moving so slowly you're acting like you're doing an inspection on it."

He swallowed a chuckle. "Just being careful. I'm carrying precious cargo."

"Precious cargo that is hungry," she said.

He drove into the back garage so she wouldn't see the other cars out front, then helped her out of the car.

"I guess it's a good thing that the doctor said the baby probably won't come until after Christmas. That means we can enjoy the holiday without worrying."

"Speak for yourself," he muttered. Zach couldn't stop worrying. He was losing more sleep with each passing night.

"What do you mean?" she asked. "The doctor says I'm totally healthy. You should rest easy and let me toss and turn," she said.

Zach, however, saw the faint shadows beneath her eyes. The doctor said it was normal for her to lose sleep, but Zach wanted Tina and the baby safe and happy. He could tell Tina wasn't at all comfortable as she grew larger with each passing day.

"Even the doctor says he thinks she's a big baby," he said.

"Hildie tells me that means she'll sleep through the night sooner," Tina said, rubbing her back as she climbed the steps from the garage.

Zach opened the door and ushered her down the hallway.

"It's so quiet," she said as they turned the corner to the den. "I wonder—"

"Surprise!" a chorus of voices called.

Tina blinked in shock at the crowd of men and women greeting her. She put her hand to her throat. "Oh my goodness, what is this?"

Keely rose and embraced her. "It's a baby shower," she said and guided her to a wing chair. "We had to limit the guest list. A lot more people wanted to come."

"I don't know what to say," Tina murmured, glancing around, recognizing some of the faces, but not all.

"I'm Sienna," a woman standing in the background said. "I'm Zach's sister. Haven't been here in a while, but I couldn't miss this."

Tina automatically stood and stretched out her arms. "Thank you so much. I can't tell you what this means. Zach," she said, glancing toward the doorway.

Zach immediately stepped forward and gave his sister a hug. "Thanks for coming. I know I've been difficult—"

"You always were," Sienna said in a dry voice. "Daniel and I had a chance to talk before the party got started, but he looks a little distracted right now," she whispered.

Zach's younger brother, Daniel, appeared totally focused on one of their neighbors, Chloe Martin. Zach remembered Daniel's past with the woman and lifted his eyebrows. "That could be interesting," Zach said in a low voice.

"You're telling me," Sienna said.

"Any chance you'll tell me what this is about?" Tina whispered.

"Later," Zach said and brushed her nose with a kiss. "You have gifts to open."

Zach slipped Tina a small sandwich before she opened the shower gifts because he knew she was hungry. He counted how many times she rubbed her back and how many times she insisted she was just fine. The correlation was one to three. Tina was not a whiner.

She alternated between princess mode and sincere delight throughout the party. A few times, she brushed tears from her eyes when she received homemade gifts of quilts, crocheted afghans and painted pictures.

He could see that she was overcome with the generosity and thoughtfulness of the attendees and it occurred to him that she truly didn't realize what kind of affect she had on people.

"I don't know what to say," Tina said, her voice breaking. "Who's the baby now?" she said as tears slid down her face. "You've all been way too generous."

"You're the generous one," Hildie said. "You just burst right in here and shook all of us up."

"We have a few more gifts," Keely said. "This one's from Ericka."

Tina opened a package of a beautiful baby carrier and a bottle of French wine. "That's Ericka," Tina said, with a laugh.

"And from Stefan," Keely said, giving her an envelope.

Tina opened it and smiled. "One round trip charter to Chantaine on Stefan's royal jet."

"I'll go," Eve said, raising her hand.

"Those tickets are spoken for," Zach said and met Tina's gaze.

Her eyes welled up with tears. "You have done too much for me. I'm humbled by your generosity. Thank you so very much."

Deciding she needed a moment to gather her emotions, Zach nodded in Keely's direction. "Time for food?"

Keely took the cue and stood, clapping her hands together. "We have all kinds of wonderful food, punch and wine. Please enjoy."

Zach took Tina to a small formal greeting room. "You okay?"

She took several deep breaths, her eyes wide. "I'm shocked," she said. "I haven't even been here that long and look at what these people have done for me. Those homemade quilts and knitted afghans must have taken hours and hours of work."

"You really don't realize the impact you've made," he said in amazement.

Her eyes filled with tears. "I also don't know if I will be staying," she whispered, clearly in agony. "I feel so guilty."

Her admission felt like a hot poker in his gut, but he refused to give in to it. This night was about Tina and the baby. Not about him. "What you've given to this community has made a huge difference. Even if you left now, we would all be changed for the better."

She took another deep breath and flew into his arms. "Oh, Zach, what am I going to do?"

This once, he wasn't going to try to tell her, because he was beginning to grasp that Tina had been pressured her entire life. She deserved the opportunity to make her own choices…even if it nearly killed him in the process.

Zach thanked everyone for coming. Daniel came to his side. "I'm headed out. Taking Chloe home."

"She didn't bring her own car?" Zach asked, gently taunting his brother.

"Okay, I'm following her home," Daniel said, shooting him a quelling glance. "Don't ask because I'm not gonna tell."

Zach lifted his hands. "Good luck and Godspeed."

Later that night, Tina nestled in Zach's arms. His strength never ceased to amaze or comfort her. She gazed out the window of his bedroom into a sky full of stars. "Did your parents love each other?" she asked.

"Huh?" he asked, half asleep.

"Nothing," she said, not wanting to bother him.

He shifted and propped himself on his elbow. "No, what'd you say?"

"I asked you if your parents loved each other."

"Yeah, they did," he said.

"How do you know?"

"They were devoted to each other through thick and thin. He would have protected her with his life. She would have done anything she could for him," he said.

"How do you know that?" she asked.

He sighed. "He worked three extra jobs when the ranch didn't bring in enough money for food or heat. He traded one of his favorite horses for a diamond anniversary band for their twenty-fifth anniversary."

"That's romantic," she said.

"She made him trade it back," he said.

Tina gasped. "Was he insulted?"

Zach chuckled. "No. She was a very practical woman. He bought back the horse and got her a new refrigerator. She was a lot happier with that."

Tina smiled and relaxed against him again. "It sounds like they had a deep appreciation for each other."

"I think they did. My father held her hand when she died," he said.

Tina's throat closed up tight. "That must have been hard," she said.

"Yes, but he wouldn't have had it any other way," Zach said. He stroked a strand of her hair from her forehead. "What about your parents? Do you think they loved each other?"

"Well, they certainly procreated," she said with a laugh. "Two sons, four daughters," she said. "I always thought their relationship seemed controlled and proper until she died. Now that I think of it, her passing may have broken his heart. He continued to rule, but then he became ill. He didn't fight it."

"My mother always said to be careful about judging other people. They might be different on the inside than they seem on the outside. Same for relationships. I had to grow up before I started to understand that," he said.

Tina thought about Zach's relationship with his former

wife. According to the outside world, he was a devoted husband, she a devoted wife. They had appeared normal, but Hildie had told her the real story had been different.

She put her hand over Zach's chest and felt his heartbeat against her palm. "After Jenny, did you decide you would never marry again?"

He paused a long moment. "Yes," he said. "But you changed my mind."

"Kiki and me," she corrected. "Would you have changed your mind if I hadn't gotten pregnant?"

"That question is irrelevant," he said. "You got pregnant."

"It's not irrelevant to me," she said, frowning.

"Stop thinking about things that don't matter. You're with me. You're safe, and our baby is safe," he said.

Tina sighed. For this moment, that was enough. She closed her eyes and snuggled against him, falling asleep.

The next morning, Tina rose early to have breakfast with Zach's sister, Sienna. Sienna had already said she needed to leave today, so Tina wanted to maximize her time with her.

"Good morning," Tina said as she carefully descended the stairs. Sienna was already seated in the den with her suitcase packed beside her. "You don't have to rush away."

"Work," Sienna said. "How are you this morning?"

"Feeling my largesse," Tina said with a laugh. "Eat breakfast with me. I'm sure Hildie has already fixed something with enough calories to feed a family of bears."

Sienna smiled. "She always did when I lived here. I'm sure she'll turn up her nose when I tell her I'm on a low-carb diet."

"I think so," Tina said as the two women walked into the breakfast room. "Morning, Hildie, you devil for deceiving me about the shower."

Hildie tossed her a look of defiance. "As if you didn't love every minute," she said.

"All of you did too much," Tina insisted.

"If you say that one more time…" Hildie said in a warning tone.

"I'm going to throw up," Sienna finished.

Tina blinked.

Hildie gave a nod of approval. "Well said, Sienna. Good to see you again. You're about five years overdue. Have a seat. Scrambled eggs, blueberry pancakes, crisp bacon and fresh fruit coming up."

Sienna groaned. "Do you know how long I'll have to do the elliptical for this?"

"Get in line. I've been doing this for months," Tina said.

Despite their protests, the two women enjoyed the sumptuous breakfast. Sienna leaned back and gestured at Tina's plate. "You didn't eat nearly as much as I would have expected with a little parasite in your belly."

Tina laughed. "Charming way of looking at pregnancy. I have to eat small meals. She keeps kicking me in my diaphragm. Little bugger."

"Ah," Sienna said with a nod. "I like the way Zach acts with you. He treats you like fine china he wants to keep from breaking. Very sweet."

Tina's smile fell. "He does that because of his first wife and how she lost the baby."

Sienna gave a slow nod. "I wasn't around for that. I tried to reach out to him afterward, but he pretty much shut me out. It looks to me like things have changed with you around."

Tina was reluctant to disclose much more. "We'll see. Tell me about your life. What made you leave Logan country?"

Sienna shrugged. "I needed to get away. Made a few mistakes along the way, but I'm better now. The city suits me. I like the anonymity."

"Is there anyone special in your life?" Tina asked.

Sienna shook her head. "Just my cat and my job, and I'm okay with that. I don't want to lose touch with you, Zach and Daniel now. I'm too busy to come home for Christmas, but maybe I can visit afterward."

"That would be great," Tina said. "I haven't made definite plans about what I'll be doing once the baby is born, but—"

"You won't be staying?" Sienna interjected, clearly shocked.

"It's a complicated situation," she said.

"Zach would die if he couldn't be near his child," Sienna said.

Tina sighed. "I respect that. I truly do, but I also want my child to see an overwhelming love between her parents. I'm not sure Zach can do that with all the loss he has experienced."

Sienna reached toward her and took her hand. "Don't count him out. You haven't seen the way he looks at you. Promise me," she said.

"I promise," Tina said. "I promise I will listen to my heart and Zach's heart if he can open up to me."

"Good," Sienna said with a nod. "I'm glad I came."

"I am too," Tina said, but she didn't want to make promises she couldn't keep.

Tina was thrilled with the success of the holiday project. Now that all the donations had been collected, invitations had been sent to the families in need of help to pick up their gifts at a community center about thirty miles from the ranch.

Zach absolutely did not want her to go, but Tina insisted. Part of the reward of the project was seeing the happiness on the faces of those who received the gifts. Plus several other people in the community had worked hard and Tina wanted to personally thank each of them.

Hildie was charged with transporting her and making sure she didn't work too hard. Joining the other volunteers gave Tina a rush of excitement. She could tell she was more than ready to get out again.

"You're doing too much," Hildie warned.

"Nonsense," Tina said as she packed donated groceries into bags for the families. "I'm loving every minute of it. Look at how happy that mother is over there."

Hildie also helped load groceries and shook her head. "I never would have expected we'd see so much donated this year since it's been a rough one for just about everyone."

"The idea is to make it easy," Tina said. "If you make it easy, then people feel successful about giving and then they want to do even more." She glanced at the clock. "Look at the time. The next group will be coming in just twenty minutes. Do you mind telling Charlene to urge people to finish with their selections?"

"As long as you get something to eat and drink," Hildie said firmly, wagging her finger at Tina.

"I'm fine," Tina insisted, exhilarated by the success of their efforts. "I'm a grown woman. I know when to eat and drink. I'll get something soon."

Somehow soon turned into later, and everything turned into a blur after four o'clock. In the back of her mind, she noticed her back beginning to hurt. She was very thirsty, but with everyone working so hard, it was easy for her to procrastinate taking a break. Tina was so busy she barely noticed when a local news team entered the distribution room.

Suddenly a microphone was pushed in her face. "Princess Valentina, how do you feel about your holiday gift campaign?"

"Tina or Ms. Devereaux is fine," she said, glancing up

from her task and suddenly feeling very tired and thirsty. "It's not *my* holiday gift campaign. It's the community's gift campaign, and everyone has done a brilliant job."

"How's the pregnancy coming?"

"My watermelon seed has grown," she said, frustrated by her sudden feeling of weakness.

"Any chance for an upcoming wedding?"

"One thing at a time," she said. "Thank you for stopping by. Did you talk to Charlene Kendricks? You really should. She's kept everything moving today."

Tina's stomach turned and she felt her knees go rubbery. "Excuse me," she murmured to the reporter. "I'm going to get a drink of water," she said, moving toward the back of the room.

The room began to tilt and sway. "All I need is water and a chair," she coached herself.

"Tina," she heard Hildie call and then she collapsed.

Chapter Seventeen

Tina awakened to a crowd of people standing over her, including a cameraman, of course. Covering her face, she groaned. Of all the things she didn't want to make the news... "Oh, please."

"She said she needed some water," a male voice said.

"We'll get that," Hildie said. "Now back off so she can breathe. You, with the camera, stop that or I'll break it. Don't you doubt for a minute that I will," she said.

"Here's some water, Ms. Devereaux," a different female voice said. "Can we find a pillow?"

"How about a stuffed animal?" someone else said.

Willing the room to stop spinning, Tina rose to her elbows. A stuffed animal was stuffed behind her back and she took a sip of the bottled water. "Thank you, Chloe," she said to the woman helping her. "I really didn't want to make a scene. I'm sure I'll catch blue blazes for this from Zach."

Chloe shot her a look of sympathy. "Those Logan men

are tough as nails," she said, catching sight of Hildie giving the cameraman a piece of her mind. "Would you like some crackers?"

"What I would like is to get away from this crowd," she said.

Chloe glanced around and waved over a few men. "Can you guys help her to the back room?"

"We can carry her if you like," one of the three men offered.

"No," Tina said. "If you could just help me stand. I'm a bit like a beached whale in my current state."

"Honored to assist, ma'am," one of the men said, and Tina prayed she didn't give any of them an injury. After she took another sip of water, they helped her to her feet and led her to a chair in an adjoining room with a door, thank goodness.

"Thank you very much," she said to the men. Chloe remained with Tina while she sipped on the bottle of water.

"Are you sure I can't get you something to eat?" Chloe asked.

Tina shook her head. "I just need to get my equilibrium back. I should have paid more attention to the signs my body was giving me, but I got caught up in the excitement. Zach is going to kill me."

"If it helps any, I fainted when I was pregnant," Chloe said.

"Really?" Tina said.

"More than once," she said.

"That must have terrified your husband," Tina said.

"Different situation. We weren't married." Chloe paused. "I was very young. He wasn't really in—" She broke off and waved her hand. "Water under the bridge now. We need to make sure you're feeling better."

Tina racked her brain for what she'd heard about the lovely

woman. "Your husband passed away, didn't he? I'm sorry for your loss."

Chloe lifted her slim shoulder. "Thank you. We were separated at the time."

"Oh, that just makes it all the more difficult," she said.

Chloe gave a wry smile. "Exactly. Now what—"

"I taught that cameraman the meaning of respect," Hildie said as she marched into the room, carrying the camera with her. Her cheeks were flushed with anger, clearly invigorated from the fight.

"Oh, Hildie, he could charge you with stealing," Tina said.

"Let him try," Hildie said. "I'll give it back. I just need to erase the memory thingy. In the meantime, we need to get you to the doctor before Zach hears about this."

"But I'm fine," Tina said.

"That's what you said earlier when I told you to eat a snack, take a break and drink some water," Hildie said in a stern voice.

"But—"

"No buts. A record number of people in this community will be having Christmas because of you. You've done enough. Now you need to take care of yourself and the baby. I've already called the doctor."

Zach walked into the ob-gyn clinic, swearing under his breath and sweating blood. If only Tina had listened to him. If only she hadn't gone to the community center. She simply didn't understand her fragility. It was past office hours. Thank goodness Hildie had insisted on getting Tina and the baby checked.

He knocked on the door to the inner office and waited, counting to ten then twenty. Finally, Hildie opened the door.

"The doctor just finished the ultrasound. Your little bugger is kicking up a storm as usual."

His lips twitched at Hildie's enthusiasm. "Do you know how this happened?"

"It's my fault," Hildie said. "I asked her to take food and water twice, then everything got busy. I'm sorry, Zachary."

He shook his head. "It wasn't your fault. You couldn't force-feed her. She just got busy and ignored her own needs. Where is she?"

Hildie pointed in the direction of a closed door and Zach knocked. The doctor opened the door. "Come in. No complications. Our mother just stretched herself a little further than she should have."

Zach met Tina's sheepish gaze. "We covered this subject this morning."

"I know," she said. "I was fine until the late afternoon crowd. I started working and forgot about taking a break or drinking some water."

Zach took a quick breath, but held his tongue. He looked at the doctor. "Any professional advice?"

"She's in excellent health, but she shouldn't run a marathon or oversee a holiday Christmas charity event without breaks."

"Please tell him the rest of the story," Tina said to the doctor. "That it's not unusual for a pregnant woman to faint and that it's not necessarily a sign of anything bad."

"True," the doctor said. "Pregnancy produces a tremendous strain on the body, especially during the later months. It's not unusual for a pregnant woman to faint every now and then."

"Not my woman," Zach said and met Tina's gaze again. "I'm taking you home and making sure you get the rest you need."

Five minutes later, he helped her into his SUV. His gut was

still twisting. From the moment Hildie had called him, he'd feared the worst. He slammed her door closed and climbed into the driver's side.

Zach wasn't sure what to say. He was still terrified that something would happen to Tina or the baby.

"It could have been much worse," Zach said as he drove out of the parking lot. "You could have fallen in a way that hurt the baby."

"The amniotic fluid is supposed to cushion the baby. With all the swelling I've had, trust me, I've got plenty of fluid," Tina retorted.

"I told you that you shouldn't go. I knew you would overdo it, but you ignored me," he said.

"This was one of the happiest days of my life," she said. "Seeing all those people accept the gifts from the community…"

"Was it worth risking your health? The baby's?" he demanded. "What if you had been permanently injured? Or the baby? Would you have been able to live with that?"

She sucked in a shocked breath and he felt her gaze on him. "Is this about me and Kiki or Jenny and the baby you lost?" she whispered.

He blinked at her blunt question.

"At some point, you're going to have to realize that I'm not Jenny and this baby is not the one you lost. I'm doing the best I can to live my life to the fullest at the same time I nurture my baby. Don't accuse me of being a bad mother again."

"I wasn't," he said.

"It certainly sounded like it," she said and looked out the passenger window.

They rode several miles in silence. Zach struggled with her accusation. He wasn't sure she knew how fragile her life or the baby's life could be, and he couldn't begin to make her understand.

Zach pulled into the garage and stopped. "Thank you for the ride home. Good night," she said and stepped out of the car and away from him.

For the next several days, Tina slept in the guest bedroom and avoided Zach at dinner. After a week passed, he approached her in the hallway late at night.

"Are you still mad at me?" he asked.

She crossed her arms under her chest. "I wouldn't use the word mad," she said, lifting her chin.

"Then what word would you use? Furious? Murderous? Beyond angry?"

"Murderous is close," she said, her sexy impudent gaze meeting his.

"Why murderous?" he asked. "All I did was drive you home from the doctor."

"While you accused me of being a bad mother," she said, her own green gaze turning dark.

"I didn't say you were a bad mother," he said.

"Close enough," she retorted.

"How could you be a bad mother when you fled all your royal crap to search out what was best for you and your baby?" he asked.

She paused a long moment. "Do you realize what I turned down?"

"I have an idea," Zach said. "Even though you were pregnant with another man's child, you could have married an English earl, an Italian count or a Spanish prince."

She appeared surprised at his knowledge. "They wanted my title. They didn't want me."

"I want you," he said.

"How do I know you don't want me just because of the baby?" she asked.

"Because I wanted you before the baby existed," he said.

She searched his gaze then looked away. "I hadn't thought about that."

"Why don't you think about it some more while you sleep with me?" he asked.

"I'm not a good sleep partner," she said. "I wake up every hour, go to the bathroom, toss and turn."

He took her hand in his and pulled her against him. "Come to bed with me."

"As long as you understand there's no sexy hootchie koo in your near future," she warned.

"No sexy hootchie koo," he agreed and reveled in her warmth. "But that's not because I don't want your sexy hootchie koo."

Tina sighed. "That's good to know."

With each day that passed, Tina felt as if she must be gaining at least a pound. Her back hurt, her thighs ached and her abdomen seemed to cramp every other hour.

"This sucks," Tina said to Hildie and Eve. "If every woman felt like I did, there would be no population explosion."

"Sit down and put your feet up," Hildie said. "You need to focus on the gorgeous baby you're going to have in just a few weeks."

"Easy for you to say," Tina said. "You don't have hemorrhoids."

Eve winced then patted Tina's hand. "I have to tell you that the assistant to the assistant of your brother got in touch with me."

"Salvadore," Tina said, astonished, but at the same time not. "Stefan wants to steal you away to manage his prize horses. What did you say?"

"Two words I learned from Zach," Eve said with a wily grin.

"What's that?"

"More money," Eve said.

Tina laughed. "Good for you. You will earn every penny if you work for my brother, so make sure you negotiate a fantastic salary. Are you really willing to live in another country to work and earn your living?"

"I'm not happy doing what I'm doing. We'll see how the Devereauxs come through."

"I should warn you that my brother is ruthless when he finds something he wants. Be careful," she said.

"I'm a big girl," Eve said. "As much as I like you, I'm not at all susceptible to a royal title. In my mind, you are the amazing exception that proves the arrogant rule."

"I'll take that as one of the highest compliments I've received," Tina said.

A week before Christmas, Tina hid in her bedroom so she could wrap the gifts she'd ordered online for Zach, Hildie, and Eve. She'd already ordered gifts for her family and Zach's brother and sister that should arrive any day.

She felt more crampy than usual but put it down to bending and stretching. Crankiness went against her usual nature, but she was also still bothered about what she was going to do after her agreed-upon time with Zachary passed.

The closer the time came for her to deliver the baby, the more she wanted to be home, but now she wasn't sure where home was for her.

A cramp twisted her muscles, momentarily stealing her breath. The intensity of it took her by surprise. *Labor?* she wondered, then pushed the possibility aside. She'd been having cramps for weeks. This wasn't any different, she told herself.

But then she felt a gush of water rush down her leg.

She gasped in shock. Her water had broken. She was in labor. She was going to have her baby very soon. Her heart hammering with excitement, she didn't know what to do first. Tell Zach. Change clothes.

She decided to change clothes and told herself to stay calm. Women did this every day. Everything would be okay. Her abdomen tightened again, this time stronger. She took another breath.

In the past two centuries of the Devereaux women giving birth, none of them had done it naturally, and she didn't plan to be the first. Right now she wanted to get to the hospital to get her epidural as quickly as possible. No need fighting the contractions.

Despite her discomfort, excitement rushed through her. *Kiki was coming soon.*

She went to the bathroom to change. As she looked at her clothes, she saw blood instead of water. Alarm shot through her. She panicked at the sight of bright red. Was her baby okay?

Tina smothered a sob. She had to hold it together. Zach would be nervous enough for both of them. Quickly changing her clothes, she grabbed a towel and went downstairs.

"Hildie," she called. "Hildie, where is Zachary? I need to speak to him immediately."

Hildie poked her head out from the kitchen. "He went out. Some calves got caught in some barbed wire. Poor animals are dumber than dirt…."

She must have read the alarm on Tina's face. "What's wrong?"

Tina swallowed over the knot of fear forming in her throat. "My water broke."

Hildie's eyes rounded. "Oh my goodness. We have to get him here right away. Call him. Call him."

"I hope he's reachable," Tina said, taking the house phone from Hildie. Zach's cell rang once, twice, three times. Her nervousness ratcheted up another notch.

"Hello," Zach said, sounding out of breath. "What do you need?"

"It's time," Tina said.

"For what?" he asked, sounding distracted.

"For you to take me to the hospital. My water broke," she said. "I need to go now."

"Damn," he said. "Hell," he said, then swore again. "I'm on my way," he said and hung up.

With trembling fingers, Tina called her doctor and was put on hold. She stepped away from Hildie, who was watching her like a hawk. Finally a nurse came on the line.

"Dr. McAllister is with a patient," the nurse said. "How can I help you?"

"This is Valentina Devereaux. I'm in labor. My water has broken." She lowered her voice. "And I'm bleeding."

"Go to the hospital immediately," the nurse said. "The doctor will meet you there as soon as you arrive."

Go to the hospital immediately. As if she were planning to go shopping or get a pedicure on the way.

Hildie walked toward her, face wreathed in concern. "Would you like some water? A cup of tea?"

"Thank you, but I'm fine. On second thought, perhaps I should take a bottle of water with me."

"I'll get it right away," Hildie said as a vehicle screeched in front of the house.

"That must be Zach," Tina said, feeling a sliver of relief. She walked toward the door, feeling another trickle run down her leg. Was it water or blood?

Determined to keep herself together, for her sake and Zach's, she carefully descended the steps. Zach jumped out of the car.

"I'll get your suitcase," he said.

He was speaking of the bag she'd packed in anticipation

of this day, but Tina didn't want to wait one moment longer. "I'd rather leave now," she said.

He stopped in his steps and stared into her eyes. She tried with everything inside her not to show her fear. He gave a slow nod. "Okay, let's go."

Hildie scrambled down the steps with a bottle of water in each hand. "Here's one for both of you," she said, shoving them at Zach. "Call me the second you have any news." Hildie turned to Tina. "You're going to do great. You're going to be fine. I know it," she said and gave Tina a tight hug. "Now go have your baby."

"Thank you," Tina said, feeling a sudden knot form in her throat, but not giving in to it. Then she slid the towel under her seat before she stepped inside the SUV.

Zach got into the driver's side and put his foot on the accelerator. "Are you in pain?"

"I'm having contractions," she said. "My water broke."

"That's why you brought the towel?" he said.

She nodded.

"That's the last thing you need to worry about," he said.

She shrugged and focused on the pavement in front of them. She felt the moisture seep into the towel. Was it blood? Why was she bleeding? She steeled herself not to panic.

She cleared her throat. "Can you please go a little faster?" she asked. "Not too fast, but faster."

She felt him shoot a look at her. "Yeah, I can do that. I'll get you to the hospital."

"I know you will," she said and felt herself grow lightheaded. *Oh, God, she couldn't lose consciousness.* Adrenaline pumping through her, she used her fear to stay awake and aware.

The contractions grew more intense and she struggled to remember the breathing techniques she'd learned during her two private prepared childbirth classes. Drawing deep breaths, she wondered if they would ever get to the hospital. The trip seemed to be taking years. She fought dizziness.

"We're close," he said.

She glanced over at Zach. His face was grim and taut. She could easily imagine what was going through his mind, the agony of his memories as his wife and son died on the way to the hospital.

Fear clutched at her. Please let her baby be okay. Please let everything be okay.

She saw the sign for the hospital and a spurt of relief rushed through her. Zach swerved into the half-circle in front of the E.R. entrance.

"Thank you," she whispered, pulling at her door before the vehicle even stopped.

"Whoa, whoa. Wait," he said, slamming the car into Park and running around to her side to help her out of the car.

As soon as she stood, Tina wove on her feet. Zach caught her against him, but he must have seen the towel on her seat. "You're bleeding."

"Sorry," she said, but the weakness she'd fought during the drive took over, and everything went black.

Chapter Eighteen

They took Tina away.

The same way they had taken Jenny away.

Zach had an ugly feeling of déjà vu. Why hadn't she told him she was bleeding? He would have driven faster. He would have gotten her to the hospital sooner.

Pacing from one side of the waiting room to the other, he checked with the receptionist twice. The hospital worker shook her head in sympathy. "I'm sorry, sir. She's in surgery. Why don't you go up to the fifth floor waiting room? Someone will give you information as soon as it's available."

Zach rode up the elevator, racking his brain for how he could have handled things differently. What could he have done to keep her and the baby safe? Maybe he should have kept a helicopter on call. Maybe he should have kept a nurse at the house.

"Mr. Logan?" a woman in scrubs asked.

He nodded, bracing himself for the worst. "Yes?"

She gave a tentative smile. "You have a baby girl. She's healthy and screaming her lungs out. As soon as we get her cleaned up, I'll bring her out to you."

Zach slumped in relief. "Oh, thank God. Thank God. Tina, she's okay, right?"

The woman paused. "Dr. McAllister is still working on her. There were complications."

His gut clenched. "But—"

"He's doing everything possible, but Miss Devereaux lost a lot of blood. She's weak, but she's fighting," the woman said and patted his arm. "I'll bring your daughter out soon."

His mind spinning, Zach sank onto the couch in the waiting room. Tina? Weak? Fighting? Oh, what if he'd lost her? What would he do?

His heart felt as if it was being ripped from his chest. His mind flashed through poignant images of the baby without her precious mother. How would little Kiki survive without her mom?

How would he?

The question shook him to the core. Tina had become as vital to him as oxygen. He couldn't imagine life without her.

He began to pray, awkward, begging prayers. He didn't want to lose her. Before he told her that he loved her.

A nurse brought his baby daughter to him. She was wrapped in a flannel blanket and wore a pink cap. He took her soft weight into his arms.

Staring into her little face, he was filled with wonder. She had Tina's lips and his hairline. Her stubborn chin might give him trouble. Oh, how he wished he could share this moment with Tina. He glanced away for a second, feeling his eyes burn with unshed tears.

The baby screwed up her face and gave a cry. Scared, he

surmised. So was he. Zach began to pace, trying to comfort his brand-new daughter and himself.

After a while, a nurse came and took the baby to the nursery. Zach waited. He paced and sat, turned off his cell phone because he couldn't bear to try to explain the situation. Hours passed and it felt like days.

Sometime in the middle of the night, he leaned his head against his hand as he sat on the waiting room sofa.

"Zachary," the doctor said.

Zach looked up, fighting fear and dread. "How is she?"

"She's had a rough time. Stabilizing her was a bit tricky, but she's going to make it. We've put her on a monitor for observation and moved her to a private room."

"I can't tell you how grateful I am," Zach said.

The doctor nodded. "Everyone was rooting for the princess. She's made an impression on this community." Dr. McAllister shook his hand. "You can go into her room, but try to let her sleep. She needs her rest. She fought hard. With the way she demanded an epidural the first time I met her, I would have never imagined her to be such a warrior."

Zach felt his spirits lift a bit. "She's stronger than she lets on. Can I see her now?"

"Of course," the doctor said.

Zach went directly to her room. The sight of her so pale, her skin matching the white sheets of the hospital bed, twisted his gut. Monitors beeped in the background. He tried not to give in to his fear, but she was so very, very still.

He wanted to touch her, but more than that, he wanted her to rest. She'd earned it. He resisted the urge to put his hand on her arm and took comfort in the steady beat on the monitor.

"Hang on, darlin'," he whispered. "Kiki and I need you. Kiki and I love you."

Sinking onto the chair beside her bed, he rested his chin

against his hands and watched over her. Looking at her, he realized she'd changed him. She'd forced him, kicking and screaming, out of his tomb of grief. She'd inspired him to look outward instead of focusing inward. She made him want to be different, better.

Hours later, a sound awakened him. He opened his too-dry eyes and saw Tina twisting from side to side. She gave a soft moan. Pain, he suspected. The nurse had told him they'd performed a C-section.

He rose and punched the call button for the nurse. Minutes later, a young man entered the room. "Hey," he said. "How's our little mama doing?"

"She seems restless," Zach said as Tina rolled her head. "Is she hurting?"

The man checked her chart and took her blood pressure. "I bumped up her pain relief so she'll rest a little longer. When she wakes up, though, she's going to feel like she's been run over by a truck."

"And my face will be the first she'll see," Zach said dryly. Zach sank back into the chair and watched over the woman who had stolen his heart.

The sun finally rose the next morning, peeking through the window blinds. Zach rubbed his beard-roughened face and stretched to get the kinks out of his back. His gaze automatically went to Tina. She still looked too pale.

Her eyelids fluttered and Zach stared at her in disbelief. She blinked again, opening her mouth as if she wanted to speak.

Zach jumped from his chair and gently touched her arm.

She stared into his eyes. "Zach," she whispered. "Our baby. Where is our baby?"

"She's fine. She's perfect," Zach said quietly, his eyes filled with tears.

She closed her eyes and tears ran down her cheeks. "She's perfect. I knew she would be."

She drifted off again before he could tell her how much she meant to him. He called the nurse to check on her and she confirmed that Tina was stable.

An hour later, Tina awakened and turned her head toward Zach. "I'm thirsty," she whispered.

He immediately rose to her side. "I'll take care of that, but in the meantime, I need you to know that I love you, Tina. More than anything. More than I ever dreamed."

Tina smiled and lifted her hand to his strong jaw.

"Marry me. We'll work out the visits to Chantaine. We can work out anything that comes our way," he said.

"I believe you," she said. "And I love you, too."

On Christmas Eve, Zach tucked Tina and their baby, Katiana Elizabeth Valentina Devereaux Logan into his SUV to bring them home. Since she'd gotten her strength back, Tina had barely been able to keep her hands off her new daughter. Every time she looked at Katiana, she was overcome with joy.

"She's the most beautiful baby I've ever seen," she said to Zach as he pulled away from the hospital with Katiana already falling asleep in her car seat.

"Yes, she is," Zach agreed, his lips twitching. "You've mentioned that a time or two, and so have I."

Tina laughed, because the fact was she'd said the same thing at least twenty times during the last few days.

"How are you feeling? Really?"

"Better. Moving around doesn't take my breath away quite as much," she said, although she knew she still tired easily. She'd quit most of the pain medication as soon as possible because she hated having a fuzzy head. "Have you heard anything from Stefan today?"

Zach had turned off the phone in Tina's room so she could rest. Since then, Stefan and Tina's sisters had been calling him constantly to check on her and the baby's condition.

"I e-mailed the photographs of you and the baby, like you asked. It was nice of you to share all the flowers you received with the other patients," he said.

"The least I could do," she said with a frown. "Think how miserable it would be to be in the hospital over Christmas."

Her comment didn't surprise him. He just hoped she would be amenable to the surprise he had waiting for her back at the ranch. Tina had told him she didn't want a big wedding, just a few witnesses. She'd also agreed that the sooner the better.

His palms itched with a trace of nerves, but he brushed them aside. "You should try and rest," he said.

"I'm too excited to get out of the hospital to rest," she said.

"Well, give it a try," he said, thinking about his plans for the rest of the day.

A little while later, he pulled toward the front of the house. Several cars were parked in the driveway.

She glanced at Zach. "Did Hildie do this? Don't tell me they're holding another shower for me."

He pulled the car to a stop and shook his head. "No, but you can be sure Hildie helped a lot." He turned to her, feeling his gut twist. "You said you would marry me."

Her eyes softened and she nodded. "And I will."

"Then you surprised me and said you didn't want to wait. You were ready to get married in the hospital."

"Well, I was. I want everything legal for Kiki and I feel like I waited forever for you to realize that you loved me."

"Well, darlin', love-of-my-life, inside our home, there's a minister waiting to do the job."

Her eyes rounded and her jaw dropped. "Now?"

He nodded. "Now. I knew you would be tied up with recovering from the C-section and taking care of the baby, so I asked Keely and Hildie if they would do the planning. Are you ready?"

Tina lifted her hand to her throat, her eyes turning shiny with unshed tears. "I am. I can't believe you did this. Why didn't you tell me?"

"I didn't want you to think about anything but getting better. If I'm moving too fast for you, then we can just have a holiday party and send the minister on his way."

"No," she said. "Let's do it. Let's make it real."

Starstuck, Tina accepted Zach's gentle assistance from the car. As soon as he collected Katiana from the backseat, Hildie rushed out the front door and down the steps. She gave Tina a big hug then turned to Zach.

"Omigoodness, she's the most beautiful baby I've ever seen."

Tina and Zach exchanged a knowing look and laughed.

"Let me hold that baby," she said to Zach. "You help your wife. Everything and everybody is ready and waiting."

After slowly navigating the steps, Tina walked past the foyer into the den. She immediately spotted Daniel, Sienna, Eve, Keely and Brent and her sister Ericka and her husband.

Tina gasped in surprise and extended her arms. "Ericka, how did you get here?"

Ericka laughed, quickly moving to embrace her. "The usual way. By jet. Of course I couldn't miss my sister's wedding after you took care of me during mine. And I got first dibs on seeing your baby. Stefan's pouting like mad. I promised to talk you into visiting Chantaine as soon as possible." Ericka pulled back and clasped her hands around Tina's. "Thank goodness you're okay. We were all so worried."

Tina greeted several of the others, then Keely introduced her to the minister, Reverend Wilhelm.

The kindly-faced man shook her hand. "It's my pleasure to meet you, your highness."

"Please call me Tina," she said, feeling her heart flutter. It was really going to happen now. She was really going to marry Zach.

"I told your fiancé that I don't perform shotgun weddings, but he insisted you were going along with this completely by choice."

She laughed at the notion of a shotgun wedding. "I am."

"Then shall we begin the taking of your vows?" he asked.

"Yes," she said. "I would like that very much."

Zach was at her side in a heartbeat, taking her hand in his. The minister led them in the promises to each other. The words and the small ceremony were important, but what was far more vital to Tina was the fact that Zach had totally opened his heart to her and that she knew he loved her and needed her. Just as she loved and needed him.

Six weeks later, after traveling across several time zones, Tina was excited to share Chantaine with Zach, Katiana, Hildie and Eve. Eve was still toying with Stefan's offer to manage the royal stables and had waited to take this trip before making such a big decision.

Hildie, who hadn't traveled farther away than Amarillo, was taking in every new experience with gusto, including a few cooking lessons from the chief chef.

Tina coaxed Zach into enjoying a day at the beach, just

the two of them, while her sisters and brothers fought over who could hold Katiana.

Zach closed his eyes as he relaxed under the beach umbrella. He slid his fingers through hers. "I could probably stomach visiting here a few times a year," he said and shot her a sideways glance.

Tina gave him a playful punch. "Yes, I know it's been torture being fed gourmet food, sleeping in that shack my family calls a palace and shooting skeet with my brother."

"Seriously," he said lifting up on his forearm. "Why would you trade this for Texas?"

"Besides the fact that *you* are in Texas?" she asked.

He gave a shrug of his strong shoulders. "I guess there's that," he said. "But—"

She put her finger over his lips. "No buts. My home is with you and Katiana. It was time for me to move away."

"Your brother still doesn't agree with that," he said and returned to his back.

"True, but did you see him melt when he held Katiana for the first time? My cranky brother turned into a complete marshmallow."

"Don't tell him that," he said.

"I'm glad we took this time out today," she said, inhaling the salty scent of the ocean and enjoying these moments with Zach. "With Stefan performing the public formalities, tomorrow will be very busy. You'll be meeting tons of people. Are you sure you're ready for it?"

"I'm ready for anything. I get to sleep with the princess at the end of the day," he said with a dirty chuckle that warmed her heart.

The following morning at precisely ten o'clock, Tina's brother Stefan gave his formal approval of her marriage to Zachary and presented Katiana as the country's newest princess. A huge crowd applauded and shouted their approval as Zachary and Tina entered the courtyard.

Katiana was in fine form, fascinated by the sparkly tiara Tina wore. Her little hand waved upward as she tried to reach for it. Kiki's face turned red and she gave a terrible frown. The baby opened her mouth to let out a yell that would have been ear-splitting if not for the sounds of the cheering crowd.

Tina made a split-second decision and pulled her tiara from her head, allowing Katiana to close her fingers around it.

Zach shook his head and chuckled. "Now I have two princesses on my hands," he said.

"Aren't you the lucky one?" she retorted.

"Damn right I am," he said and took her mouth in a kiss.

* * * * *

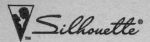
Silhouette®

COMING NEXT MONTH

Available October 26, 2010

#2077 EXPECTING THE BOSS'S BABY
Christine Rimmer
Bravo Family Ties

#2078 ONCE UPON A PROPOSAL
Allison Leigh
The Hunt for Cinderella

#2079 THUNDER CANYON HOMECOMING
Brenda Harlen
Montana Mavericks: Thunder Canyon Cowboys

#2080 UNDER THE MISTLETOE WITH JOHN DOE
Judy Duarte
Brighton Valley Medical Center

#2081 THE BILLIONAIRE'S HANDLER
Jennifer Greene

#2082 ACCIDENTAL HEIRESS
Nancy Robards Thompson

SPECIAL EDITION

REQUEST YOUR FREE BOOKS!
2 FREE NOVELS PLUS 2 FREE GIFTS!

SPECIAL EDITION
Life, Love and Family!

YES! Please send me 2 FREE Silhouette® Special Edition® novels and my 2 FREE gifts (gifts are worth about $10). After receiving them, if I don't wish to receive any more books, I can return the shipping statement marked "cancel." If I don't cancel, I will receive 6 brand-new novels every month and be billed just $4.24 per book in the U.S. or $4.99 per book in Canada. That's a saving of 15% off the cover price! It's quite a bargain! Shipping and handling is just 50¢ per book.* I understand that accepting the 2 free books and gifts places me under no obligation to buy anything. I can always return a shipment and cancel at any time. Even if I never buy another book from Silhouette, the two free books and gifts are mine to keep forever.

235/335 SDN E5RG

Name	(PLEASE PRINT)
Address	Apt. #
City	State/Prov.	Zip/Postal Code

Signature (if under 18, a parent or guardian must sign)

Mail to the Silhouette Reader Service:
IN U.S.A.: P.O. Box 1867, Buffalo, NY 14240-1867
IN CANADA: P.O. Box 609, Fort Erie, Ontario L2A 5X3

Not valid for current subscribers to Silhouette Special Edition books.

Want to try two free books from another line?
Call 1-800-873-8635 or visit www.morefreebooks.com.

* Terms and prices subject to change without notice. Prices do not include applicable taxes. N.Y. residents add applicable sales tax. Canadian residents will be charged applicable provincial taxes and GST. Offer not valid in Quebec. This offer is limited to one order per household. All orders subject to approval. Credit or debit balances in a customer's account(s) may be offset by any other outstanding balance owed by or to the customer. Please allow 4 to 6 weeks for delivery. Offer available while quantities last.

Your Privacy: Silhouette is committed to protecting your privacy. Our Privacy Policy is available online at www.eHarlequin.com or upon request from the Reader Service. From time to time we make our lists of customers available to reputable third parties who may have a product or service of interest to you. If you would prefer we not share your name and address, please check here. ☐

Help us get it right—We strive for accurate, respectful and relevant communications. To clarify or modify your communication preferences, visit us at www.ReaderService.com/consumerschoice.

HARLEQUIN®

A Romance

FOR EVERY MOOD™

Spotlight on

Inspirational

Wholesome romances
that touch the heart and soul.

See the next page
to enjoy a sneak peek from
the Love Inspired® Suspense
inspirational series.

*See below for a sneak peek from
our inspirational line, Love Inspired® Suspense*

*Enjoy this heart-stopping excerpt from
RUNNING BLIND
by top author Shirlee McCoy,
available November 2010!*

**The mission trip to Mexico was supposed to be an
adventure. But the thrill turns sour when Jenna Dougherty
and her roommate Magdalena are kidnapped.**

"It's okay. I'm here to help." The voice was as deep as the darkness, but Jenna Dougherty didn't believe the lie. She could do nothing but lie still as hands slid down her arms, felt the rope around her wrists.

"I'm going to use a knife to cut you free, Jenna. Hold still."

The cold blade of a knife pressed close to her head before her gag fell away.

"I—" she started, but her mouth was dry, and she could do nothing but suck in air.

"Shhh. Whatever needs to be said can be said when we're out of here." Nick spoke quietly, his hand gentle on her cheek. There and gone as he sliced through the ropes on her wrists and ankles.

He pulled her upright. "Come on. We may be on borrowed time."

"I can't leave my friend," Jenna rasped out.

"There's no one here. Just us."

"She has to be here." Jenna took a step away.

"There's no one here. Let's go before that changes."

"It's dark. Maybe if we find a light…"

"What did you say?"

"We need to turn on the light. I can't leave until I know that—"

"What can you see, Jenna?"

"Nothing."

"No shadows? No light?"

"No."

"It's broad daylight. There's light spilling in from the window I climbed in through. You can't see it?"

She went cold at his words.

"I can't see anything."

"You've got a nasty bruise on your forehead. Maybe that has something to do with it." His fingers traced the tender flesh on her forehead.

"It doesn't matter *how* it happened. I'm blind!"

Can Nick help Jenna find her friend or will chasing this trail have Jenna running blindly again into danger?

Find out in RUNNING BLIND, available in November 2010 only from Love Inspired Suspense.

FROM #1 *NEW YORK TIMES*
AND *USA TODAY* BESTSELLING AUTHOR

DEBBIE MACOMBER

Mrs. Miracle on 34th Street…

This Christmas, Emily Merkle (just call her Mrs. Miracle)
is working in the toy department at Finley's, the last
family-owned department store in Manhattan.

Her boss (who happens to be the owner's son) has placed
an order for a large number of high-priced robots, which
he hopes will give the business a much-needed boost. In
fact, Jake Finley's counting on it.

Holly Larson is counting on that robot, too. She's been
looking after her eight-year-old nephew, Gabe, ever since
her widowed brother was deployed overseas. Holly plans
to buy Gabe a robot—which she can't afford—because
she's determined to make Christmas special.

But this Christmas will be different—thanks to Mrs.
Miracle. Next to bringing children joy, her favorite activity
is giving romance a nudge. Fortunately, Jake and Holly
are receptive to her "hints." And thanks to Mrs. Miracle,
Christmas takes on new meaning for Jake. For all of them!

Call Me Mrs. Miracle

Available wherever books are sold
September 28!

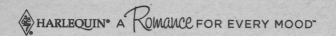

HARLEQUIN
RECOMMENDED READS
PROGRAM

LOOKING FOR A NEW READ?

**Pick up the latest Harlequin Presents® book
from *USA TODAY* bestselling author
Lynne Graham**

THE PREGNANCY SHOCK

Available in November

Here's what readers have to say about this
Harlequin Presents® fan-favorite author

"If you want spark and a heart-thumping read,
pick up any of Lynne's books....
I can never get enough of her intense stories."

**—eHarlequin Community Member Katherine
on *The Greek Tycoon's Defiant Bride***

AVAILABLE WHEREVER BOOKS ARE SOLD

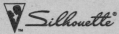